Deadly Bargain

You Get What You Pay For

Other books by
Brenda M. Spalding

The Green Lady Inn Mystery Series
Murder and mystery with a touch of spooky
Broken Branches
Whispers in Time
Hidden Assets
The Spell Box
Bottle Alley

Visit Florida
Blood Orange
Honey Tree Farm
The Alligatar Dance

Deadly Bargain

You Get What You Pay For

A Detective Max Harlow Mystery
by
Brenda M. Spalding

Dedicated to all those who believe
in me and hold my hand.

Chapter One

Two men rolled up to the second-hand shop and removed an overstuffed upholstered wing-back chair from their van. Struggling, they pushed it in the door.

"You sure this a good idea?" the younger man asked.

"I think it's the dumbest idea ever, but the boss said there are too many eyes on him for a straightforward delivery."

The men put the chair down and the one in charge barked to a young man behind the counter. "Here is the chair that Mr. Smith will be coming to pick up. It's a special order. For no one else."

"Yeah, yeah," the teen replied, head down, clicking away on his phone.

"Are you listening to me?" the big man shouted.

Startled, the teen looked up, brushing his sandy blond hair out of his eyes. The boy stared at the strange man with a Russian accent and a large hook nose. He also noticed the man's arms and neck were covered with what he guessed were Cyrillic tattoos.

The young man, Chris Metcalf, thought the man resembled the Russian mobsters he saw on the TV. His phone pinged with a message from one of his friends, distracting him again .Chris worked at his father's consignment shop on Saturdays. He hated missing out on time with his friends at the beach.

"Remember what I told you," The older of the two men said. The younger man stood there, unsure of what he should do.

"Tell your dad that Mr. Smith is coming to pick up this chair later this afternoon. This is an arrangement your father is aware of. Only Mr. Smith must claim the chair. Are you listening to me? This is important," The man apparently in charge shouted.

Chris jerked his head up, "Yeah, I'm listening. Only Mr. Smith." Young Metcalf went immediately back to his phone messages.

The man left the upholstered wingback chair in line with three other upholstered chairs and walked out the door. Getting into his truck, he looked back into the second-hand shop window and saw the kid still playing with his phone. Shaking his head, he punched in his boss's number.

"I'm not so sure this is a good idea, Sergi," Misha said. "That kid watching the shop has as much brains as those little annoying gnat things that bite me."

"It'll be okay, Misha. I'm calling Mr. Smith to get him to pick it up right away."

Misha didn't like leaving the chair with the kid. The chair was very valuable to his boss, but he didn't argue with his brother-in-law. Ever since Sergi Melnikov married his sister, things had gone from bad to worse.

Sergi spat out the window as he slammed the van into gear and pulled out, spinning the gravel and shells out of the second-hand shop parking lot and onto Tamiami Trail.

Bert's Beach Bargains occupied a dusty corner of a strip mall in Osprey, just down the Tamiami Trail from the $3 million-dollar high-rise waterfront condos and sidewalk restaurants of Sarasota. The rich who didn't work and their trust-fund kids dropped off their used items for the not-so-rich to recycle and breathe new life into.

On the Gulf Coast of Florida, the area was home to several arts and cultural schools and performing arts centers, from the Ringling Mansion and Circus Museum to the purple-roofed Van Wezel Performing Arts Center.

Bert's Beach Bargains did a brisk business buying and selling to the coastal community. Special orders were not a regular part of their business. Bert wondered about it at the time, but money was money and boy, did he need it.

Chapter Two

Bert Metcalf struggled in the back door with a tattered box of mix-matched glassware and two old oil paintings he'd picked up from a garage sale. Bert was 62, balding and overweight. His wife desperately tried to control his eating to keep him alive. He dropped the bag of fast-food burgers and fries he held in his teeth on the counter. He called to his son. "Chris, lend a hand here, will ya, please?"

"Chris, you hear me?" Metcalf yelled.

Chris, at seventeen, was not interested in spending his Saturdays in his father's musty, smelly shop. He planned to hit the Siesta Key Beach with friends. Chris grabbed the box from his father, placing it not too gently on the counter. His father cringed at the sound of glass breaking.

"Watch it. That's money in there."

"Yeah, right," Chris moaned, grabbing a ten from the cash box and striding out the door. Hopping into his beaten-up Ford Focus, he spun out of the parking lot onto the Trail, headed to the beach and his friends on Siesta Key, perennially one of the Top Ten Beaches in America. Stopped at a red light, it dawned on him that he forgot to tell his dad about Mr. Smith coming to pick up the chair that somebody left for him.

Oh well, he'll figure it out, Chris thought, turning up the radio and drumming out the rhythm on the steering wheel. Chris couldn't understand his father's fascination with other people's old cast-offs. The junk didn't bring in all that much money. Other parents had real jobs and could afford to buy their kids great cars and go places and do things. Chris had plans. He wouldn't slave for his father forever. Sarasota Community Technical College offered some neat courses he was looking at that would give him a career in something much better than a dusty, smelly old second-hand shop. Maybe something to do with computers. Chris could picture himself making the next big thing in video gaming.

Chapter Three

It was eight o'clock that evening when Sarasota Police Senior Detective Max Harlow and his partner Sgt. Lou Markowski arrived outside the small shop in the waterfront retirement mecca of Osprey. The flashing lights from their vehicles lit up the parking lot, casting a rainbow of colors in the puddles left from a late evening rain.

The detectives passed an ambulance idling, waiting for orders to take someone living or dead somewhere.

Harlow noticed the Medical Examiner's van parked off to the side. Dr. Clair Murphy was already inside. Murphy and Harlow had an excellent working relationship. After his divorce, Murphy became his companion for the police functions he felt obliged to attend. Harlow enjoyed her company, and they both understood the claims the jobs had on their lives. Lately, he'd been thinking of asking her out for a meal. Harlow told himself it would not be an actual date. Just two colleagues who had to eat.

Harlow endured divorce two years ago. Murphy's husband had died several years ago. It seemed natural that they should attend such functions together.

He shelved those thoughts for now as he walked ahead, looking around. "Who's the officer in charge?" Harlow asked a young patrol officer.

"Perez caught the call. He's inside, waiting for you with Murphy," Gleason answered.

"Shit, not that moron."

Gleason was startled, "Who, Murphy or Perez?"

"Perez, of course." Harlow knew Sgt. Perez was the laziest person he had ever run into as a cop. How he got to be a detective in the Robbery and Homicide Division was anyone's guess.

Chapter Four

Harlow and Markowski donned blue paper booties and disposable nitrile gloves at the doorway and walked inside to meet Sgt. Perez and the ME.

Harlow nodded to Perez. "Hey, Murphy." Clair bent over the victim, her assistant photographing close-ups of the injuries and the cords that bound the victim to the death chair.

Harlow asked Perez, "Any ideas what went down here?"

"It's just like you see it. My guess is a robbery gone bad. The robbers thought the old guy had money stashed. He wouldn't tell them where it was." Perez always looked for the easy answer.

Detective Harlow had not spent nearly thirty years on the force looking for easy answers. This was more than a garden variety robbery.

The victim, Bert Metcalf, was tied to an old wooden kitchen chair. He'd been beaten and tortured to death. Blood had pooled in glossy dark stains on the floor around the legs of the rickety chair.

"What's your take on this, Murphy?" Harlow said.

"I'll know more when I open him up. Right now, I don't see any injuries that look life-threatening. He was beaten but you just don't kill someone right before you get the answer you're looking for." She stood, straightening the kinks in her back, giving Harlow a quizzical look. Harlow loved the way her mind worked, always looking a little bit deeper.

"Good, later then," Harlow said. Murphy and her assistant packed up to take Bert Metcalf out to the van for his last ride to the morgue.

Harlow stood in the middle of the second-hand shop and played, *what's wrong with this picture?* Metcalf had been murdered, and he saw three upholstered chairs that had been ripped to bits, stuffing thrown all around. Tilting his Panama hat up and rubbing one of his cigars in his fingers, Harlow saw what might be evidence of yet a fourth chair.

Back in the shop office, paperwork and what he presumed were receipts were tossed around like confetti.

Harlow knew this was more than your every day robbery.

"I can hear the wheels turning. What do you think happened here, Max?" Markowski asked.

Perez stood by, looking bored.

Harlow stepped back, swaying on his heels, thinking. In his late fifties, losing his hair and with an expanding waistline, Harlow wondered whether he was ready to retire this year. He'd seen humanity at its worst and many strange things in his time. This was high on the list. In the back of his mind, he had a couple of ideas whirling around.

"Those other chairs were torn apart. If I was to guess, there was supposed to be something in one of those chairs. And when it wasn't there, someone beat the hell out of Metcalf. They killed him, either accidentally or on purpose, trying to find out where that something was."

"You've got to be kidding me," Perez shouted.

"Harlow, you're reaching again. It's a straight-up robbery. What could anyone want in a sleazy second-hand shop like this except hope for a few dollars?" Perez strutted, gesturing wildly. "It was probably some North Trail crackhead who got carried away and went too far. End of story. Case closed."

"Perez, you are one lazy motherfucker." Harlow shaking his head, watching Perez sputter and fume.

"I'm going to report you. You can't talk to me like that."

"I just did," Harlow said. "And Perez, I want every shop owner and employee in the area on both sides of the Trail questioned about what they might have seen. Who they saw coming and going and what time. I want the report on my desk in the morning."

Perez closed his eyes and swore under his breath. Then he shrugged. He'd get a couple of rookies knocking on doors to canvas to satisfy Harlow and be done with it.

The detective knew Perez was a lazy bastard. Harlow would send a couple of his squad around as well.

Harlow found Mrs. Metcalf crying on a worn wooden bench in front of the store, a woman officer by her side. Detective Harlow looked and shook his head.

"Poor woman," Harlow said, tipping his worn Panama hat and snuffing out his cigar. He motioned to the officer.

"Hello, detective. I'm family liaison officer, Patricia Gleason.

"Leave us for a few minutes, please," Harlow asked.

Addressing Mrs. Metcalf, Harlow sat beside the weeping woman. "Mrs. Metcalf, can you tell me how you found your husband tonight?"

"I was worried when Bert didn't come home for supper. He wasn't answering his cell or the shop phone, so I drove down to check. The door was unlocked. I found him in there tied to a chair and beaten. How could they? I haven't been able to reach my son, either. He usually works here on Saturdays."

"Thank you, Mrs. Metcalf. I'm sorry for your loss. We will be talking to you again.

Harlow gestured for Officer Gleason to return.

Walking away, he called, "Come on, Markowski, let's wait and see what Murphy, our friendly coroner, can tell us about how Metcalf died. I don't expect any surprises there. We need to talk to their son when we find him. He might know something."

Harlow turned back to Mrs. Metcalf. "I'm sorry, ma'am. We need to talk to your son. Any idea where he might be?"

"He's usually at Siesta Key Beach with his friends on Saturday. I've tried calling, but it goes straight to voicemail." Mrs. Metcalf tried to pull it together but was losing the battle. Officer Gleason handed her more tissue to blow her nose and wipe her eyes.

"Sorry I can't be of more help. Bert was such a gentle soul. I can't believe why anyone would do this to him."

"Office Gleason will take you home, and we can talk tomorrow after you've had time to process all this. Maybe something will come to you by then." Harlow helped the distraught woman to stand and watched Gleason drive away.

"I'll send a couple of cars out to Siesta Beach looking for his car," Markowski said, punching numbers into his phone.

"Yeah, and I want to hear what Murphy says about the autopsy. This guy went through hell and back, and I want to know why."

Chapter Five

Harlow and Markowski tried to get Julia Metcalf's statement while sitting in the Metcalf home.

"I'm sorry for your loss, Mrs. Metcalf, but we have to reach your son, Chris. You said he was working at the shop yesterday."

Chris Metcalf was still nowhere to be found. His mother had tried his mobile phone several times, but it kept going directly to voicemail.

"Yes, Chris hates working in the shop. My son's young and wants to be off with his friends hanging out at the beach or whatever they do. I can't believe he turned his phone off, but he always forgets to charge it."

"Does he usually stay out all night?"

"Yes, he does. Not often, but he usually calls me to let me know. I'm worried he hasn't called." She suddenly stopped. "What if something has happened to him, too?"

"We'll find him. We have patrol cars out looking for him."

Harlow hated this part of the job. "I know this is stressful, but just a couple more questions. There were three upholstered chairs ripped apart like someone was looking for something. Do you know anything about those chairs?"

Mrs. Metcalf stopped and thought. "Burt had three old chairs there for a couple months. He was expecting another one to be delivered. It was unusual. A special order, which we don't do." She stopped to reach for a glass of water. Her statement had caught Harlow's interest. A second-hand consignment shop with a special order, three chairs sitting in the shop for months, and a fourth was missing. Where was missing chair?

"Can you tell me anything about this fourth chair?"

"We were eating dinner. Yeah, that's right. It was last Thursday night. This man called and said he had a small reupholstering business in Osprey. Well, you can imagine my husband is all confused about what that has to do with our shop. But this guy carried on, saying he has to go out of town, and one of his customers wanted this chair desperately."

"Did your husband give you this man's name?"

"He did later that evening. He said it was something Russian, he thought." Mrs. Metcalf paused, trying to remember the name. "Mr. Romanoff, yes, that's it a Mr. Romanoff."

Markowski wrote the name down and would look it up.

"I still don't see how you ended up with the chair."

"Mr. Romanoff said that his customer, someone named Mr. Smith, would pick the chair up on Saturday afternoon from our shop, and we could earn a little $50 commission. It sounded weird, but we needed the money. Our shop is not doing all that well. I don't know why this man chose to leave the chair with Bert. He could have left it with any number of other shops."

"One more question before we leave. Does your husband keep records of who buys and sells what in the shop? You know, so that he can track the

13

consignments?" Harlow was putting things together, and if he was right, the fourth chair was still out there, and someone was willing to kill to get it.

Chapter Six

The following morning, Harlow was again called out to Bert's Beach Bargains and greeted by flashing lights from several police units in front of the small consignment shop. Perez was walking around, barking orders that were largely ignored.

"What's up this time, Perez?" Harlow said.

"The store was broken into sometime last night. Nothing was taken that Mrs. Metcalf can determine, but the office is a mess. Someone had a field day with the paperwork." Harlow had the urge to throttle the insensitive idiot. Perez was one lazy son of a bitch who somehow had climbed the ladder out of Patrol into the Robbery Division.

"Shit," Harlow exclaimed softly. He and Markowski pushed past Perez and found Julia Metcalf sitting on the office floor, shuffling through piles of papers.

"Mrs. Metcalf, I'm so sorry. Take a seat at the desk. Can we get you water or something?"

"Thanks, Detective. I'm sorry, what was your name again?"

"I'm Detective Harlow, and this handsome fellow is Detective Markowski."

Markowski chuckled at that because no one in

their right mind would ever call him handsome. His Polish and Jewish ancestry had done a number on his features, leaving him with a tall, thin frame, a prominent nose, bushy eyebrows, and the need heavy, black-framed glasses that called attention to his creeping hairline.

"Is there any way you can dig through all this and find out who Bert might have sold that chair to?" Harlow indicated the papers strewn on the scarred wooden floor. Most were handwritten receipts and invoices. He noticed an old unused computer collecting dust tucked into a corner.

"Your husband didn't use the computer?"

"I don't think he ever turned it on. Bert always made little notes in a ledger as well as receipts. Give me a few minutes." She went to a file cabinet and flipped through a couple of folders.

Harlow browsed through the shop while Mrs. Metcalf searched the cabinet and paperwork, looking for her husband's ledger.

Harlow noticed a sofa that showed little wear. The one he had now at home was stained and worn. Maybe it was time to replace it. Since his divorce, he had done little to the condo he owned off Bahia Vista, where the Amish community met working-class Latinos and folks just down from New York to restart their life in paradise. So long as he had the bare necessities, he was happy. He visited his two kids as often as his ex-wife and his workload allowed. It was his devotion to work that led to his divorce in the first place. Not every woman is cut out to be a cop's wife. Always on call: nights, weekends, and holidays. He didn't blame her.

"I got it," Julia Metcalf shouted from the back. "I found a note in the ledger from yesterday for one upholstered chair."

Harlow put down the baking dishes he would never use and looked to see what she had found.

She handed him a handwritten ledger and a page for one upholstered chair sold to Arthur Faraday and gave his address on Ben Franklin Drive in Sarasota.

"That's a pretty upscale address for someone slumming at a consignment shop," Harlow said.

"Not really. We get all kinds of bargain hunters here. Some college kids look to furnish on the cheap or the seniors who can't afford new stuff. You never know. Some of the wealthier around her shop for the bargains too. The more money they have, the more they haggle on the price."

"Thanks, ma'am," Harlow said, preparing to leave, "We'll be in touch."

"Any word on my son yet?" she asked, tears welling in her bloodshot eyes.

"We're still looking. Sorry. If you hear from Chris, let us know straightaway."

Chapter Seven

Markowski signaled that Harlow had a call. "It's from your girlfriend Murphy at the coroner's office."

"Sorry. I have to take this. We'll talk later." Harlow and Markowski left Bert's Beach Bargains. Standing in the shell parking lot, Harlow half-listened to what Dr. Murphy was saying as he watched an old Ford Focus pull up. A young teen boy hurriedly climbed out.

Chris Metcalf looked stunned at all the police in the parking lot. He was wearing the same Bermuda shorts and long tee-shirt over his tanned body he wore on Saturday. Long sun-bleached hair hung around his face.

"What happened? What's going on?" the young man asked frantically.

Harlow disconnected his call with Murphy, "Later." Of course, he'd get an earful from Murphy for hanging up, but this was important.

Harlow looked at Markowski and shook his head in disbelief.

"Chris, Chris Metcalf?" Harlow asked.

"Yeah. Who are you?" Chris asked with the arrogance of youth.

Harlow flashed his badge. "Detective Harlow of the Sarasota Police Homicide. My partner Detective Sergeant Markowski."

"Why are you here? What's happened?" Chris yelled, pushing past the officer,s and rushing into the shop. "Dad, Dad!"

Mrs. Metcalf heard her son's voice and dropped the vase she was putting on a shelf. The sound of the glass shattering across the floor echoed through the sad store. She ran out and grabbed her wayward son. "Oh my God, Chris." She hugged him tight, then pushed him away. "Where the hell have you been?"

"I was out with Sammy and the guys. My phone died. I didn't think you'd mind. No big deal."

Harlow and Markowski followed them back into the store and waited for Chris to explain where he had been for two days.

His mother burst into tears and collapsed onto a nearby sofa. "No big deal?" She whispered. "Right, no big deal." Raising her voice, shouting, "The cops have been looking all over the place for you. But you couldn't find a phone anywhere to call and let me know you were okay. I thought someone had killed you too."

Chris stood in shock, his mouth hanging open. "What do you mean, *killed me too*?"

"Chris, I hate to tell you, but your father is dead. They killed him here at the store yesterday."

"This can't be real," Chris said, sinking onto the sofa beside his mother.

Harlow told Markowski to call Officer Gleason again to stay with Mrs. Metcalf and Chris for a while. It would take them a long time to come to grips with all this.

Chapter Eight

Detective Harlow brought Chris Metcalf to the downtown station to get a statement. Julia Metcalf was too distraught to deal with Chris and more questions. The detective could always question her again later.

Chris was fidgeting, sitting in the bare, freezing interview room across the table from Harlow. The boy was nervous and upset. He was playing with the remains of the paper coffee cup he had torn to bits.

"Chris, what you can tell us about Saturday? You were at the shop with your dad, right?"

"I was, and I wasn't," Chris said, staring at the mess he had made. His eyes were full of unspent tears.

"What do you mean by that?" Harlow asked, trying to be patient. *God, I hate teenagers. They have a language all their own and are loaded with attitude. Is this what I have to look forward to with my kids?*

"I left as soon as Dad came in with a load of junk from a garage sale. He runs all over town to those damn sales on Saturday mornings."

"What time was that?"

"About 3 o'clock, I guess."

"Did you get a delivery of an upholstered chair that afternoon? Your mom said there was something about a special delivery."

"Yeah. This weird guy came by and left this hideous chair. He said to hold it for Mr. Smith and no one else. He put it with the other chairs."

"Go on."

"I was texting my friends. You know, trying to make plans and not paying a lot of attention because it didn't seem that important. The guy said to give the chair to Mr. Smith, but I was in a hurry to get to the beach. I forgot to tell my dad."

Chris suddenly looked Harlow in the eyes. "Oh, my God. Do you think that's what got my dad killed? Over a stupid chair?" It finally hit home.

Harlow felt terrible for the kid, but one forgotten message did indeed get his father killed. Another thought crossed his mind. The whole thing started with the phone call from this guy Romanoff about a chair. If Metcalf had only said no or asked more questions, he would still be alive.

"Chris, I don't think it was the chair itself. I think it was what was hidden in the chair."

"I don't get it."

"Chris, we think that there might have been drugs or something else illegal in that chair. That something was supposed to go to this guy, Mr. Smith. When Mr. Smith came to collect it, and it wasn't there, they beat your father to find out where the chair went."

"So, it was my fault," Chris said, tears running down his face. He swiped the remains of his shredded coffee cup off the table, all his teenage bravado gone.

Harlow closed his eyes, leaning back in his chair. *All this because a teenager didn't pass along a message. A kid can be such a pain in the ass.*

Chapter Nine

Max Harlow and Lou Markowski pushed through the steel doors to the Medical Officer's autopsy room. The cold of the space hit him immediately, and the smell of antiseptic and blood assaulted his nose.

Murphy glared at Harlow, holding a scalpel and Bert Metcalf's liver in the other hand.

"I called to give you an update on the Metcalf murder. You do know I'm swamped here. I don't appreciate being hung up on."

"Sorry, Chris Metcalf chose that exact moment to show up at the store."

"Okay, I get it." Murphy put down the liver and scalpel and ripped off the heavy blue protective gloves she wore. Picking up a clipboard, she read out the report on Metcalf.

"He died of a heart attack. No surprise there. He was headed towards a triple bypass in the next few months, if not a fatal heart attack all on his own. Metcalf might have survived the beating, but his heart gave out first."

"If he died before he could tell them who had the chair, someone is still looking for it, right?" Harlow leaned against one of the stainless-steel sinks. "Whoever did this is vicious and willing to kill anyone to get what was in that chair. I'm betting it's worth a lot of money and very illegal."

Murphy tore off her blue plastic protective gown, balling it up and tossing it in the trash. "I guess we need to find it before there is another victim."

"You got that right," Harlow said, shaking his head.

Harlow hesitated before asking, "Murph, you got time for a cup of coffee? Or a drink after work?" He was not quite sure why he asked her, but glad he finally did.

"Sure, Max," Murphy said with a question in her eyes. "You Okay?"

"Yeah, I'm fine. I'd just like a bit of company. Some things are harder to deal with than others."

Chapter Ten

The parking lot at Duffy's Grill on University Boulevard was half empty at 7 o'clock when Detective Harlow pulled his SUV in and parked beside Dr. Murphy's Miata.

The place was not a cop hangout, so maybe they could keep their friendship discrete. The last thing he needed was a lot of station gossip. Duffy's wasn't far from the heavily traveled I-75 and the golf course and polo communities that so many coveted in Sarasota. Harlow didn't have the money on a detective's salary nor the patience for either one.

Opening the door for Murphy, Harlow said, "Glad you could make it." He noticed that she had changed out of her usual scrubs and into a fashionable pair of dress pants and a pretty, blue top. Murphy even wore sparkly earrings that set off her gray hair, looking feminine and attractive. He caught the whiff of flowery perfume, and for a moment, he felt human. He wondered why he had waited so long. She sure didn't look like a coroner now. He raised an eyebrow and cocked his head as he followed Murphy into the noisy restaurant.

"Do you have a quiet table somewhere?" Murphy asked, nodding to the ball game on the widescreen over the bar.

The server showed them to a table away from the TVs blaring the latest Tampa Bay Bucs football.

"I guess she figures were not here for the sports," Murphy said.

"She's a smart lady," Harlow said, picking up a menu.

Looking around the casual bar and discussing the options to Okay a few minutes. They ordered a couple of drinks and simple meals. Harlow ordered a bacon cheeseburger with his beer. Murphy opted for a grouper sandwich after she made sure it was really going to be grouper. So many restaurants were substituting cheaper fish for the Florida native.

"So... What's up, Harlow?" Murphy asked, toying with her silverware.

"To be honest, I don't know." Silence followed for a heartbeat before he went on. "Yes, I do. That guy Metcalf. He did nothing wrong, and yet they killed him. He left a wife and son. It got to me. All at once. I know I screwed up my marriage. I worked way too much. Oh, I know it's all part of the job. I missed so much of my kid's life. But, Jesus, Murphy, I'm lonely. I needed to be with someone tonight." He stopped talking and looked forlornly at Murphy.

She reached across the table and squeezed his leathery hand, and said nothing at all.

"That's why I like you, Murph. You listen. I can't believe I just unloaded all that on you."

"I like you too, Max. Next time, I'll do the unloading, okay?"

Their dinners arrived in time to break up the awkward moment. They spent a pleasant evening talking about their jobs, the routines, and sharing bits of cop shop gossip until both of their phones rang at the exact same time and jolted them back to the present.

Answering the calls, Harlow and Murphy quickly hung up in unison.

"You headed to Ben Franklin Boulevard?" Harlow asked.

"How'd you guess? Anyway, thanks for dinner and the company. I did enjoy it, Max."

"My pleasure," Harlow said, putting his credit card on the check. "I hope you don't mind me talking your ear off from time to time."

"Anytime."

"Meet you at the scene," Harlow said, tipping his hat.

Taking their separate vehicles, they rushed through the traffic on the Ringling Bridge, around St. Armands Circle to another murder.

Chapter Eleven

Detective Harlow and Dr. Murphy had driven in their separate vehicles, not wanting to fuel the office rumor mills. They arrived on Ben Franklin Drive and followed the blue flashing strobe lights to the crime scene.

A young officer in the lobby directed them to the scene upstairs on the fourth floor, unit 426.

They were met by Sgt. Markowski. "Wow, Doc. You look great. You have a hot date that got interrupted?" Markowski asked, with a wink and a grin.

"Keep your insinuations to yourself," Harlow muttered.

"Max, your favorite dick head from Robbery Division is already in there," Markowski said, nodding inside.

What Harlow could see of the two-bedroom condo was tastefully furnished in transitional style. The colors were muted blues and gray with fashionable sea scenes hanging on the walls.

"Shit," Harlow said, rolling his eyes and grimacing. "and, I had such a pleasant evening so far," looking in Murphy's direction. He chuckled softly to himself when he saw Murphy blush. Together the three donned protective booties and gloves, ready to walk into the latest tragedy in Sarasota, the town they called America's Most Livable City.

Perez met them at the door. "Aren't you a little overdressed for the occasion, Dr. Murphy?"

"Not that it's any of your business, but I was out for the evening when I got the call. Can I see the body, please?" Murphy didn't wait for an answer, pushing past Perez.

"Well, Perez, you going to tell me? Or do I have to guess what happened here?" Harlow said.

"Yeah, yeah. Two guys live here. A couple of queers. One came home and found the other shot dead."

"Perez, you're an insensitive prick. They're people just like you and me and should be treated with dignity," Harlow said. Perez bristled with rage.

"It's murder now, so get the hell out of here. You need to take some sensitivity training classes." Harlow was fuming and not going to let this rest. He'd have a word with the captain in the morning. Harlow had enough of Perez and wanted something done. It wasn't the first time he complained about how Perez conducted his investigations.

Harlow ran his fingers through his sparse, graying hair as Perez stormed out.

Murphy kneeled over the body, examining it. Another man in his late sixties sat on a couch beside Officer Gleason. Harlow guessed he was the dead man's partner. He noticed the man was sharply dressed in a button-down shirt and neatly pressed Dockers. His tasseled loafers shined.

Harlow nodded to Gleason to get her attention and motioned her over. "We meet again. So, tell me."

"The deceased is Daniel Brookmeyer. The man over there is Arthur Faraday. They were life partners and have lived here together for the last ten years. He came home to find the door partway open. He knew

28

Daniel would never leave the door open like that. Faraday called out, and when he got no answer, he entered and found his friend as you see him. Faraday managed to call 911. Sorry detective, but he's a wreck."

"Thanks, Gleason," Max said, taking the scene in. He didn't want to question Faraday, considering his state, but he had a job to do. Getting shot between the eyes was an indication of something more sinister than a simple robbery gone wrong. And why pick on this guy?

Chapter Twelve

"Mr. Faraday, I have a few questions. Was Mr. Brookmeyer having any problems that you know of?"

"No, none." Faraday sniffed and blew his nose in the tissues he held. Tossing the ratty tissues aside, he tore a fresh one from the box, squared his shoulders, closed his eyes for an instant. "Okay, I'm ready."

Faraday was sixty-something, tanned, and in reasonably good shape. His hair was gray and showed a recent cut at a good barber.

"Did Daniel have any business that might have made enemies? Did you two have large amounts of money here that someone might have found out about? Any relatives that we could contact?"

"No, Daniel retired about eight years ago, the same as me. We had a small printing company and invested well enough to let us live comfortably. We don't have large amounts of cash lying around. What we have is in the bank or investments. In case you are wondering, Daniel and I were married as soon as the laws changed. They changed here in Florida in January of 2015. We got married on Valentine's Day that year."

"Mr. Faraday, Daniel was alone until you came home tonight. Where were you coming from?"

"It's Daniel's birthday next week. I've been planning a surprise for him. He likes a certain style of furniture and he's wanted a chair for that corner over there. I'd been shopping around for a few weeks."

Faraday gestured to space in a corner by the windows overlooking Sarasota Bay. The window captured the Intracoastal Waterway view, the barrier islands like Longboat, Lido, Anna Maria, and the Gulf beyond the expansive windows opening onto a small balcony.

"He had been looking for just the right piece to place there, and I found what I thought would be perfect in a second-hand shop. I picked it up yesterday, but the upholstery color was horrible. So, I brought it to be recovered in something more suitable today. I was so afraid Daniel would find the chair in my SUV. I would have been here with Daniel except for stopping to drop off the chair. I can't believe anyone would want to hurt my Daniel. He was such a gentle soul and would never hurt anyone." Faraday broke down and sobbed. Gleason was also moved to tears as she put her arms around the man to comfort him.

Max turned to his partner. "Lou, we need to find out where that chair is. I'm betting it's the same one from the Metcalf murder. What the hell is so special about that chair?" the detective wondered.

Chapter Thirteen

"Misha, you dummy, wake up. The cops are leaving," Sergi pounded and shook his partner.

The two men had been sitting in the car outside the condos waiting what seemed like hours for the cops to leave. From their vantage point at the edge of the parking lot, they had a clear view of the entrance. Lights from the patrol cars flickered against the façade of the luxury condo on the edge of the bay. They watched as the police came and went, followed by the coroner van.

"What are we going to tell Mr. Smith? We still don't have that stupid chair of his. I knew it was a crazy idea. He'll go nuts if we go back without the stuff." Misha ran his hands through his dark hair, dragging his palms down his face and groaning.

"Let's think about this," Sergi said. "The guy in there didn't know what we were talking about, right? No chair. He said he was not Faraday. So, Mr. Faraday must know where the chair is."

"It's not my fault you got scared and killed this Brookmeyer guy. We could have waited there for Faraday to arrive. But no, you just had to shoot him with your big noisy gun, and we had to get out of there," Sergi countered.

"Not my fault," Misha shouted. "You were yelling, pissed off, and saying you were going to kill him anyway. I didn't mean to pull the trigger. It just went off."

"Funny, you managed to hit him right between the eyes?"

"You scared me into doing it," Misha cried.

Sergi looked out the car window and the cops pulling away. "Shut up and let me think."

They watched one of the patrol cars pull away with a man sitting in the back with a woman police officer.

"Now Mr. Smith will kill us, you fucking idiot," Sergi yelled.

"Wait." Misha jumped in his seat, hitting the dash with both hands. "The cops had a man about the same age as the guy in the condo. He was in the back of the car when they left. I bet that's Faraday."

"Sometimes you do get a bright idea." Sergi was excited and trying to form a plan.

"I know, I know," Misha cried. "He must have dropped the chair off somewhere before going home. So, we wait outside the police station. Pick Faraday up and make him take us to the chair," Misha said. He was proud of himself for coming up with something that might stop them from getting killed.

"You know, dummy, that might just work," Sergi said, giving Misha's head a friendly shove. "You better not fuck this up, or I'll kill you myself."

33

Chapter Fourteen

Markowski walked Faraday out of the police station in downtown Sarasota. "We'll be in touch, Mr. Faraday. Thanks for your statement. We'll send someone around to the upholstery shop to pick up the chair in the morning. I know this has been stressful for you. Dr. Murphy will make arrangements for you to claim Daniel's body."

Arthur Faraday stifled a sob, blew his nose on his initialed handkerchief, and stuffed it in his pocket. "Thank you, officer, and thank Detective Harlow for me too. You have all been very kind. I must be going now. I have the unpleasant duty of informing Daniel's family. I've called for an Uber."

Markowski and Faraday shook hands. Markowski turned to the parking garage at the back of the station, and Faraday waited at the corner for his Uber driver to appear.

When a black late-model sedan pulled up, Faraday thought nothing of hopping in the back seat and giving the driver his Ben Franklin Drive address. Leaning back in the seat, Faraday closed his eyes, thankful for the cool of the car's leather interior. He just wanted to wake up and find this was all a horrible nightmare.

At the stoplight at the end of the block, a strange man yanked the back door open and jumped in beside Faraday. "Sorry fella, this ride is taken," Faraday told the man. The stranger was wearing a leather jacket over a black shirt, and dark sunglasses covered his eyes.

"I'm afraid it's my ride, and you're coming along," Sergi grinned, jamming a .38 into Faraday's ribs.

This set Faraday to crying again. "This can't be happening. All I wanted to do was give Daniel a birthday present."

"Oh, it's happening alright, and you're going to tell me where that birthday present is," Sergi said, making his point by waving the gun in front of Faraday's bloodshot eyes.

"Yes, yes, don't hurt me," Faraday mumbled. "It's off Washington Boulevard, not far from here, but they're closed by now. The police are going to pick up the chair in the morning."

"In that case, we are going pay that shop an unexpected after-hours visit. Now Mr. Faraday, give my friend here the directions."

Chapter Fifteen

Misha Kalashnik and Sergi Melnikov drove to the small upholstery shop off Orange Avenue, parking in the alley behind the building. All the shops were closed for the night. There were few streetlights and even fewer security lights in the rundown industrial area trying to make a comeback on the city's northern edge where wealth gave way to poverty.

"I told you it was closed," Faraday chanced a comment.

"We have a special key," Sergi said, brandishing a crowbar. He strode to the back door.

Misha stood beside Sergi. "What that hell do you think you're doing?"

"We are breaking in, you moron," Sergi said, shaking his head.

"And what do you think our friend there is going to do as soon as we're inside?"

Misha wrinkled his brow and looked from Sergi to Faraday still sitting in the car and shrugged his shoulders. "I don't know."

"He'll run for the cops if you leave him there, dummy. Go get him." Sergi wedged the crowbar against the lock and heard it pop. He turned to see Misha drag the protesting Faraday out of the car.

Sergi could hear Misha muttering about being called a dummy. If he weren't his wife's brother, he'd shoot him himself.

Entering the shop, Sergi took out a flashlight and splayed the light around, looking for the missing chair.

"Hang on to him, Misha. Find something to tie our friend here up with for now. Try that work area back there."

Misha poked Faraday in the back with his gun and shoved him towards a table strewn with hand tools and remnants of cut-up leather and fabric. Rummaging around, Misha found some heavy cord, ordered Faraday to sit on the floor, and tied his hands and feet.

"Look, you don't have to do this. I know you are smarter than that other guy gives you credit for," Faraday whispered so that Sergi would not hear him.

Misha paced around the shop, holding the gun in one hand and running the other hand through his hair. "Sergi is my sister's husband. I don't think she knows all he does and where his money comes from. She thinks he is a legitimate businessman." Misha sneered and spat out the words. "She wanted me to work with Sergi to learn to be a businessman. My sister doesn't know the kind of business her husband does. She closes her eyes."

"I don't think you meant to kill my Daniel, did you?" Faraday whispered. He was hoping there was something decent still left in the man in front of him.

"I had to," Misha said. "He saw us and could identify us. I panicked. Sergi was shouting and yelling to do something to make him stop talking about calling the police. The next thing I knew, your friend was on the floor, and the gun was in my hand."

"What's your name?" Faraday felt a glimmer of hope, but he had to hurry. He could hear noise from the shop — the sounds of ripping, banging, and cursing.

"Misha," the man said, waving his gun. "But don't get any ideas. I'm not going to suddenly be your pal."

Sergi appeared, dragging a large, heavy bag. "Come on. You know what you have to do. I'll put this in the car."

Faraday's heart sank. Did he get through to Misha? He closed his eyes and heard the door to the shop slam shut and waited for the bullet to his head. The thought that he would soon be joining his beloved Daniel raced through his brain.

I'm coming, Daniel. I loved you in life. I'll love you in death.

Misha took packing tape from the bench and wrapped a piece across Faraday's mouth. Misha looked at Faraday, shook his head, raised his gun, and fired.

Sergi heard the shot as he was lifting the heavy bag into the sedan trunk. "The boy finally got some balls," Sergi muttered, grinning and thinking that Mr. Smith would not be trying to kill either one of them today.

Faraday slowly opened one eye at a time, astonished he was still alive. Then, he looked surprised and wide-eyed at Misha, who shrugged and slugged him upside his head, knocking the old man out cold.

Misha opened the passenger side door and slid in.

"It's done," he mumbled, hoping they might find a way out of this after all. He wasn't a killer at heart. He prayed he didn't hit Faraday too hard.

"Good. No loose ends, remember," Sergi said. The car sped out of the alley, bouncing off a trash dumpster and nearly hitting one of Sarasota's many homeless residents. The tire rubbed against the dented fender making a scraping sound.

"Whoa, that was close," Sergi laughed. "Almost one less beggar on the streets of Sarasota."

My wife is going to kill me for wrecking her car, thought Misha.

Chapter Sixteen

Detective Harlow pulled up beside Markowski's cruiser outside the upholstery shop. Arthur Faraday was being treated by EMS and was strapped to a gurney to be transported to Sarasota Memorial Hospital.

Harlow stepped out of his car, dousing his cigar in a puddle left from the overnight storm, and motioned Markowski.

"How the hell did Faraday end up here?" Harlow asked.

"I walked him out of the station after he gave us his statement. He was going to wait for an Uber to take him home. That's all I know."

"Why didn't you drive him back to his place?" Harlow said, annoyed that Faraday could have been the next casualty in this mess.

"He seemed fine and had already called for a ride. We both wanted to get home, and he didn't want company. I felt he needed time to be alone and take in the loss of his partner." Markowski told his boss. He knew that Faraday getting hurt was his responsibility, realizing now that he should have had a patrol car drive him home.

"You couldn't have known what would happen.

But it remains: how did Faraday end up here?"

Harlow held his hand up and stopped the EMS techs from closing the ambulance doors.

He asked the driver, "What can you tell me?"

"Your victim here took a nasty knock on the head. The owner of the shop found him when he opened up. They're inside waiting for you. Mr. Faraday has a concussion, at the very least. Unfortunately, he hasn't regained consciousness. The sooner we get him to the hospital, the better."

"Thanks. I'll check with SMH later to see how he's doing."

Harlow stood watching the ambulance drive away with the siren blasting. He rocked back and forth on his feet, hands in his pockets for a moment, his thoughts racing. *Faraday must have been grabbed and brought to the shop by whoever killed Daniel Brookmeyer. The killer was looking for the chair and whatever was in it. Did they find what they were looking for? And why did they let Faraday live?*

Markowski knew how Harlow's mind worked.

"You ready to go inside, Max?" Markowski prodded him.

Harlow brought his mind back to the present. "Yeah, yeah, let's see what they can tell us."

The scene inside the shop reminded the detectives of Bert Metcalf's Beach Bargain Shop. The skeletal remains of an upholstered chair was torn apart, fabric and stuffing all over the floor.

A small Hispanic man shuffled out of a back office to greet Harlow and Markowski. Extending his hand, he introduced himself. "Carlos Ruiz, the owner. I can't tell you how distressed I was when I came here this morning."

"Yes, Mr. Ruiz, walk us through this morning from the time you arrived," Harlow said. Markowski took out his notebook.

"When I arrived, the back door was open. It had been forced. I couldn't imagine what anyone would want to steal in the shop. We don't keep any money here." Ruiz walked around to where the ruined chair rested.

"The first thing I saw was this mess. Mr. Faraday bought it in to be reupholstered. Whoever picked out the original fabric must have been colorblind." Ruiz picked up a remnant from the floor and shuddered at the psychedelic design.

"I turned to go to the office and call the police when I saw poor Mr. Faraday lying over there by the workbench. I called 911. I hope he will be alright."

"Thank you very much, Mr. Ruiz. You have been very helpful. My partner, Sgt. Markowski will take your formal statement. I want to look around for a few minutes if you don't mind."

"No, go right ahead. Whatever I can do to help."

Harlow left Ruiz with Markowski and wandered around the small shop to study the scattered chair remnants.

Rocking on his feet, studying the chair, he noticed something odd. At first, he thought it might be fine sawdust, but bending down, he dabbed a bit on the tip of his finger. What he found was definitely not sawdust.

Chapter Seventeen

"I'll see you back at the station, Lou. Going to check in with Murphy first. See if the hospital can give you any idea when we can talk to Arthur Faraday," Harlow said. He stood beside his unmarked car, reaching in his pocket for a cigar. He tipped his battered Panama hat back, watching a plane high in the sky. Sarasota-Bradenton International was nearby. SRQ to locals. It was a small, easy-to-navigate airport, not like Tampa, where you had miles between terminals. The aircraft was probably on its way to some exotic location: Cancun, the Caribbean, Rio. Someday, maybe soon, he'd be flying. Until then, he had a murderer to catch.

As soon as he turned on Washington Boulevard toward the ME's office, he called Claire Murphy.

"Hey Murph, you got time for a coffee?" Harlow asked.

"I'm rather busy, but I can take a few minutes if you can stand the lunchroom coffee," she said.

"It'll do. I'm more interested in seeing you than the coffee anyways."

"Wow, that's quite a statement from you, Max."

"Don't go getting any ideas. Just want to bounce some ideas around, is all. I have Lou busy with something else. I'm almost there. See you in a few." Harlow hung up to navigate the traffic thru Sarasota and down Tamiami Trail to Siesta Drive to the ME's office attached to the morgue.

Harlow knocked on Murphy's open door. "You have time for that coffee?"

"Sure, what's bugging you, Max?" Murphy asked, getting up and following Harlow down the hall to a small staff lunchroom. Murphy checked the coffee pot, made a face, and tossed the contents in the sink.

"I'll make a fresh pot. It'll only take a minute." Talking with her back to Harlow while she fixed the coffee, Murphy asked, "So what drags you down to the land of the dead, Max?"

"I know that what happened to Bert Metcalf and Daniel Brookmeyer are related to whatever was in that chair."

"Wait, you said *was*," Murphy interrupted him.

"Yeah, we found the remains of the chair at a shop along with Arthur Faraday this morning. The chair had been ripped to shreds. Faraday was tied up and struck cold on the head. He's at the hospital now."

"Oh, the poor man. He seemed like a sweet soul."

Harlow produced a plastic evidence bag out from his pocket and slid it over the table to Murphy. "I found this substance on the floor by the chair. Can you get one of your techs to analyze this?"

"This is the idea you wanted to bounce off me? You think that it's cocaine."

"It would explain a lot."

Murphy poured them coffee, fixing Harlow's the way he liked, three sugars and creamer.

"Murph, I've been thinking," Harlow said, staring into his cup.

"Oh, no, now what?"

"I've been thinking about retiring. This job is getting to me. I don't see my kids. They're getting older, and I'm missing it all. I don't want to be a stranger to them. Besides, there are things I want to do, places I want to go. I watched a plane take off from SRQ and thought I'd like to be on it. At the same time, what would I do with myself with all that extra time? I'm a cop, have been for over twenty-five years. Playing golf is just not me."

"Max, I understand. I felt the same way when my husband died. I didn't have kids, but I wanted to do things with my life. I almost quit this job, walking away after twenty years. Then a young girl was found murdered by Sapphire Shores. She needed me." Murphy reached across the table to squeeze Harlow's hand.

"Max, Bert Metcalf, and Daniel Brookmeyer need you now. You can always put in your papers after you catch their killers, if you still want to. Just give it some more thought before you throw in the towel. Besides, who would I go for drinks and conversation with?" Murphy smiled, releasing Harlow's hand.

"Thanks, Clair." Harlow stood, put his cup in the sink, and left the lunchroom.

Murphy sat there stunned for a moment. Harlow had never called her by her first name before.

Chapter Eighteen

Harlow's mobile phone rang as he climbed into his car. He left the door open and the engine running with the A/C to release some Florida heat.

"What you got, Lou?"

"Faraday is groggy but awake and able to talk. The doctors will let us in for a few minutes," Markowski told him.

The officer was sitting in the visitor waiting room near Faraday's room. He watched the doctors and nurses as they came and went caring for Faraday. A patrolman was stationed outside the room. Markowski worried that there could be another attempt on the man's life once the killer found out Faraday was still alive.

"On my way. Has he said anything yet?" Harlow said.

"Yeah, he said he should have bought retail."

"I guess it wasn't much of a bargain at that." Harlow hung up, cursing as an out-of-state snowbird cut him off. "Why can't you people figure out where you're going? Or stay the hell home in Michigan."

Sarasota Memorial Hospital was a rabbit warren of corridors. Even after getting Faraday's room number and directions, Harlow wasted several minutes finding his way.

"Faraday say anything else?" Harlow asked his partner as he finally found the right room. Slightly out of breath, the detective leaned against the wall, blaming his love of a good cigar and the occasional whisky in the evening. Of course, the extra fifty pounds around his middle didn't help.

"No, the doctors say he had a subdural hematoma and concussion. It's a case of wait-and-see if he comes out of it. They may have to operate to release the pressure on his brain. Sometimes it resolves on its own. Their brain guy is on his way in. He was on vacation in Key West."

Markowski's phone chirped. He stepped away to take the call. Harlow quietly entered Faraday's room. He was astounded by all the tubes and lines attached to the pale man lying in the bed.

Dragging a chair over, Harlow sat beside the bed. "Come on, old man. You have to wake up and tell us who did this to you."

The detective was developing a soft spot for Faraday. The man was trying to do something special for his partner, suddenly lost him, and ended up fighting for his life. It just wasn't fair. A bargain from a consignment shop had brought so much pain to so many people.

Markowski motioned from the hallway, "Max, we got a lead."

"What?" Harlow asked.

Walking through the hallways to the parking garage, Markowski explained about the call.

"One of the patrols working with the homeless picked up a man who said he had information on what happened at the upholstery shop. The homeless guy says he was rummaging in a dumpster behind the shop when this car almost ran him over. The car hit the dumpster, so there should be some trace evidence.

Maybe we can find the make and model."

"That's the best news I've had all day," Harlow said. "Let's go see what else he can tell us."

Chapter Nineteen

Harlow and Markowski stood outside the interview room and looked through the glass at the man inside.

A young officer had brought the man in after hearing his story about the incident at the upholstery shop.

"His name is James Lilly. I've seen him hanging around the streets for a couple years now. He usually finds a bed at the Salvation Army on 10th Street in the cold weather. If you're going in there, you might want to wear a gas mask. He's pretty ripe. I'm having the patrol car fumigated," the officer said. Making a face, he walked away.

Harlow inhaled a deep breath and opened the door to the interview room; the odor hit him; his eyes watered.

Markowski, behind him, tried to cover his nose and mouth. "You've got to be kidding me?"

"Sorry, it's been a while since I've had a shower," Lilly said. "Guess I do smell a bit." He pulled the front of the neck of his tee-shirt out and sniffed himself. Lilly was about thirty years old but looked fifty. He was dressed in casual homeless attire of second-hand camo pants and a worn tee-shirt. At least a couple of weeks' worth of scraggly beard covered much of his face. The man showed the ravages of living on the streets.

"A bit? Mr. Lilly, you reek," Harlow said. "I'll see to it that you have a hot shower and meal before you leave the station. Anyway, I appreciate your coming here today."

"Thanks," Lilly mumbled. "The showers at the Salvation Army are always busy. I don't like to use them."

"Tell me about the car that almost hit you," Harlow said.

Lilly settled back with the coffee placed in front of him. "I was dumpster diving behind the shops. You never know what you might find. The upholstery shop throws out large pieces of fabric I can use for pillows, a mattress, ground cover, all kinds of great stuff."

"I get it. So, then what happened?"

"I heard a gunshot."

"Wait, you heard a gunshot? How do you know it was a gunshot?"

"I served in Afghanistan. Marines. So, I know what a gun sounds like." Lilly sat back and crossed his arms over his chest.

Harlow could see the light go out of Lilly's eyes, and the memories of his time in that war zone flood in. So many of the Florida homeless were veterans suffering from PTSD.

"The man we found at the shop was not shot, so that's interesting. Lou, have the techs go back and look for a bullet near where we found Faraday," the detective asked Markowski.

"Back to the car, Mr. Lilly," Harlow said.

"This dark sedan was parked behind the shop. I didn't pay much attention to it. This first guy came out lugging this bag and tossed it in the trunk. Then I heard the gunshot. The guy smiled, slammed the trunk, got in, and started the engine.

"Then this second guy came running out. He looked like he'd just killed his best friend. He jumped in the passenger side, and they speed out of there. Like I said, they almost hit me and sideswiped the dumpster."

"You think you can identify either of these men?" Harlow said.

"It was pretty dark back there, but yeah, I can try."

Harlow left the room and instructed a waiting officer to help Lilly get a shower and a change of clothes. "Find him something decent to eat too, not just a hamburger either. Set him up with a six-pack photo lineup. See if he can pick anyone out. If not, get a sketch artist in here. We can bring what Lilly finds to Faraday to see if he can add anything." Harlow left, tossing three twenty-dollar bills at the officer.

Markowski followed Harlow outside. The detective stopped on the sidewalk, rocking on his heels. "Lou, why a gunshot and no one is shot? Why would a gunman look like he killed his best friend? Call the hospital. See if Faraday is awake yet and talking. Then get those techs to check on that dumpster. I want answers, and I need them now."

Chapter Twenty

After checking with the hospital, Markowski returned to the crime scene at the upholstery shop to look it over again with the techs. Detective Harlow needed to see Clair Murphy again. When done with the techs, he headed directly to morgue.

When Harlow rapped on the window, Murphy was leaning over a body on the table, looking intently at an older man's insides.

Murphy motioned Harlow to wait a minute. "John, can you dissect the heart and lungs for me? I'll be right back." She instructed her assistant, pulling off her gown and bloody gloves.

"In my office," Murphy said, leading Harlow down the hall.

"I got the results back on that powder you found. I'll tell you. It was quite a surprise. It's something new around here, but I've been hearing about it for a while now."

"You going to tell me, or not?" Harlow said, taking a seat and crossing one leg over a knee. He pushed his hat back and a pulled a cigar from his breast pocket.

"Don't you dare light that smelly thing in here."

"I wouldn't dare." He'd long realized a cigar in his hand, even an unlit one, was a coping mechanism and nervous habit. He returned it to his pocket with a pat.

"Okay. The powder or, more accurately, crystal, is what the dealers are calling Flakka. It's a combination of heroin and crack or heroin and methamphetamines. It's a new generation version of a type of synthetic drug called bath salts."

"Shit, my wife used bath salts all the time," Harlow exclaimed.

"It's not the same thing but the same name. I'm still researching it, and it looks cheap and lethal. If this drug gets out widely, it will be a full house down here."

"Christ, what a mess." Harlow stood and paced the small office. "Let me run this by you."

Sitting behind her desk, Clair could see the wheels turning in Harlow's head.

"We have a chair left at Bert Metcalf's shop on the South Trail for this Mr. Smith person to pick up. I don't believe for a minute that is his real name."

"I agree. That's got to be a false name," Murphy said.

"Right. Metcalf sells the chair to Faraday and gets killed because of it. The drug dealers return to the shop to find out who bought the chair."

"We know they have to be dealers because of the substance you found, and I was able to identify as Flakka, aka bath salts."

"You're a quick study, Murph," Harlow said, smiling. He sat again and leaned over his knees. "They kill Daniel Brookmeyer because he didn't know what they are talking about. Then, somehow these perps kidnap Faraday right after we talk to him. They force him to take them to the upholstery shop where the chair is. I'm still wondering why Faraday is alive when our witness James Lilly heard a gunshot."

"I have an idea," Murphy said. "What if one of the guys was supposed to kill Faraday, but chickened

52

out? Maybe Faraday talked him out of it. So, this guy slugs Faraday instead of shooting him. I bet he didn't mean to hurt him as bad as he did."

"You might be onto something, Clair. We have two men, the one in charge, giving the orders. And the other one following the orders. He doesn't want to be there and might be growing a conscience." Harlow jumped up and rounded the desk, taking Murphy by surprise. "You are brilliant," he said, kissing her quickly and rushing out, dialing Markowski. Dr. Clair Murphy sat there, wide-eyed and stunned. *Could something more be developing between her and the irascible Detective Harlow?*

Chapter Twenty-One

Harlow met up with Markowski outside Arthur Faraday's hospital room.

"He's awake. The doctors say we can have a few minutes."

Easing open the door, Harlow observed Faraday sitting up with his eyes closed. "Hello, Mr. Faraday. Are you able to answer a few questions for us today?"

Faraday twitched, looked at the detective and nodded, pushing his half-eaten breakfast tray away. "I don't have much of an appetite."

"Hospital food is not that appetizing at the best of times. Like us to bring you something from the outside?" Harlow said.

"That's very nice of you to offer, but no, thank you. Maybe if I'm still here in a couple days and getting desperate," Faraday joked.

Harlow sat next to Faraday's bed. "Tell us how you ended up at the upholstery shop."

While Markowski scribbled notes, Faraday told the detectives how he mistook a dark older model Toyota for his Uber ride. He directed his kidnappers to the upholstery shop, where they tied him up. He was held at gunpoint by a man called Misha.

Markowski interrupted, "Did this Misha have an accent?"

"Yeah, but not that strong. It could have been Russian, definitely Eastern European. I think he had been in this country for a while. Maybe since childhood," Faraday said. "I've heard that accent on some of the TV shows."

"Then what?" Harlow said.

"The other man, I don't think I heard his name, left us. I could hear him tearing and throwing things around. I figured these men would kill me like they did Daniel when they found whatever it was they were looking for. So, I talked to Misha. Appealed to him to let me go."

"Apparently, it worked," Harlow said.

"I guess. Anyway, Misha fired the gun. My ears rang. I thought he shot me, but he didn't. The next thing I remember is waking up in the hospital. The doctors said I had been hit in the head and had a concussion and a brain bleed. I don't understand."

"It looks like he slugged you with the butt of the gun a bit harder than he intended. I think Misha only wanted to knock you out so they could get away. He probably had orders to kill you. You are a lucky man you tickled his conscious. If they find out you are alive and you can identify them, your life could still be in danger."

"I might be able to identify the one called Misha, but I'm not too sure about the other guy. My brain is still pretty scrambled."

Harlow stood and put his hand on Faraday's bony shoulder. "I'm glad you're doing better. If you remember anything else, let us know. There is an officer outside your door, just in case."

A nurse came in to take Faraday's temperature and blood pressure. "Sorry, detectives, time's up. Mr.

Faraday needs his rest."

On the way out, Harlow stopped to talk to the officer guarding Faraday's room. "I want you to be extra careful who goes into this room. From now on, you check ID badges. No badge, they don't go in. Pass it on to whoever relieves you. Mr. Faraday is a VIP from now on," Harlow said.

"Roger that."

Walking to the garage, Harlow expressed his concern about Faraday's safety to Markowski. "If the man who wanted Faraday killed finds out that he's alive, Faraday's life be in danger. And the accomplice who let him live in the first place, too. We have a name, Misha. A place to start looking."

Markowski leaned over the roof of the car before getting in. "You never told me what Murphy identified about the stuff you found on the shop floor."

"Right. It's called Flakka, aka bath salts. It's commonly made up of a combination of heroin and crack cocaine or heroin and methamphetamines. Murphy said it is a new designer drug on the streets over the last couple of months. Cheap to make. And lethal."

"Jesus, as if we didn't have enough of a drug problem with the normal shit out there," Markowski said.

"We need to shut this down before it gets out of control."

Chapter Twenty-Two

Back at the station, Harlow called his crew together for a briefing. "We have a new synthetic designer drug hitting the streets." He scrawled *Flakka* in big letters on a whiteboard.

An officer in the back raised his hand, "What's that, boss?"

Others nodded and mumbled.

"Lou can tell you all about it in a minute. Dr. Murphy is researching it. We'll let you know more."

Harlow continued writing. "We need to find a Russian or Eastern European named *Misha* who has been in the country long enough to lose most of his accent. He's working with another man, maybe as an unwilling partner. They are driving a dark color, late model Toyota that has front end damage from hitting the dumpster outside the upholstery shop," Harlow said.

Markowski picked it up. "Check with body shops for a late model Toyota with front passenger-side damage. Maybe stolen. Something has to surface."

Harlow printed another name on the board: *Mr. Smith.* "This name was given as the person who was to pick up the chair from Metcalf's shop. I believe that whoever made the drug, concealed it in the chair, then left it at the consignment shop for Mr. Smith, the dealer, to pick up and distribute. When that didn't go as planned, that's when bodies started to drop in Sarasota."

Harlow wrote the name *Faraday* on the board. "Arthur Faraday has seen both of the killers. He can identify them. As long as they are at large, his life is in danger. We have to catch these two perps and fast. Next, we have to ID Mr. Smith and intercept these drugs before they flood our streets. That's it for now. Let's get it done."

Chapter Twenty-Three

"Misha, you fucking idiot," Sergi screamed. Misha and his sister Anya came running from the kitchen. Sergi was pacing, running his hands through his hair. "Do you know what you have done? Or should I say, haven't done?"

Throwing down the paper he had been reading, Sergi walked up to Misha and knocked him to the floor. "It's on the front page of the Tribune." Sergi picked up the paper to read it to Misha. "A Sarasota man, Arthur Faraday, was found unconscious in Carlottie's Upholstery Shop. The police are following several leads as to who broke into the shop and why Mr. Faraday was there. The victim is recuperating in Sarasota Memorial Hospital, suffering from a severe concussion."

Misha lay on the floor, rubbing his jaw. "I couldn't do it, Sergi. I killed his friend. By accident, if you remember."

Sergi stood over a terrified Misha. "You have got to fix this. Get your ass down to that hospital and finish the job."

Sergi threw the newspaper at Misha and stalked out of the room, slamming the door so hard the windows rattled.

Anya helped her brother to stand. "I don't want to know what is going on here. You and Sergi are up to something, and I don't want any part of it."

Anya followed Sergi and left the room, pulling her phone out of her pocket and punching in a number.

Chapter Twenty-Four

Terrified about what he was sent to do, Misha strolled into the hospital, carrying a huge bouquet in front of his face. He didn't want to be picked up on any surveillance cameras.

He stopped at Reception to find Faraday's room number and directions, shaking with dread about what he was there to do.

Questions raced as he took the elevator up to the fifth floor. *What if someone asks why I'm here? Do I really have to do this? Will Mr. Smith, whoever that is, kill Sergi and me if I don't? Could Faraday identify us? Would he identify me? After all, I didn't kill him the first time.*

The elevators doors opened, and he was hit with the quiet sounds of monitors beeping and nurses shuffling back and forth.

Misha carried his flowers higher to hide his face and followed the numbers on the wall to find Faraday's room.

Moving slowly down the corridor, he peeked into the rooms he passed, seeing patients hooked up to wires and IVs. Nurses passed him as they hurried along with their duties, not giving him a second glance

.   He began to relax a bit until he saw a young policeman sitting in front of Faraday's room.

"Oh shit," Misha whispered to himself. "I can't do this. Sergi is going to kill me himself."

He crept closer to Faraday's room. He wanted to see what condition the man was in. A nurse breezed past him and entered the room, calling, "Hello, Mr. Faraday, how are you today?"

Misha listened to the pleasant banter between the nurse and Faraday, who seemed to be recuperating well.

"Oh, this is not good," Misha mumbled, retracing his steps. Misha left the flowers at the nurses' station and fled the hospital.

On the way back home, he came up with a story to tell Sergi that might just keep him alive.

Chapter Twenty-Five

Detective Harlow and the men and women in his squad worked through the night to find any car that might match the suspected Toyota.

The detective yelled across the room, "Boss, I might have a lead on the car. A repair shop in Bradenton said a 2018 Toyota was brought in this morning with dam-age to the front passenger side."

Harlow took a breath. He was exhausted. At his age, he struggled to run on an empty tank. Finishing his cold coffee, he yelled back, "Send me the address," as he stormed out the door, waking up Markowski on his way.

"Come on, Sleeping Beauty. We found the car."

Markowski raised his head off his desk, "Right with you, Max," he groaned.

Harlow drove while Markowski dozed. He steered down US 301 and turned onto MLK Boulevard in Bradenton, looking for the shop along 5th Street. Pulling into a lot crammed with cars in varying states of repair, Harlow shook Markowski. "You going to join me today? I'm a hell of a lot older, and if I can stay awake, so can you."

Markowski grunted and groped for the door latch. Finally, he found it, stumbled out of the car, and caught up with Harlow. "Sorry, boss, I haven't pulled an all-nighter in a while."

In the corner of the garage sat a 2018 dark blue Toyota sedan with a banged-up passenger side. The front bumper was scraping against the tire, which was about to blow if it didn't get changed too. It could be the car they were looking for. Markowski jotted down the license plate number and the VIN.

A man came out of the office wiping his greasy hands on a shop cloth. "What can I do for you, fellas? I'm Gary Winters, the owner."

"Detective Max Harlow from Sarasota Homicide Division, and my partner, Detective Sgt. Lou Markowski. That car out there might have been involved in two murders and attempted murder." Harlow pointed to the Toyota. "Can you tell us who brought it in and when?"

"Yeah, I'll get the paperwork." Winters walked back into his office. Harlow followed him.

His back to the detective, talking over his shoulder, he shuffled papers on his desk, "These two guys brought it in late yesterday. I told them it would take about a week for the repairs. Gotta order a front quarter panel and a whole new headlight fitting, and a new tire. One man did all the talking and said he didn't want to claim it on his insurance. Some don't, if they're going to keep the premiums down."

Back in the garage, Markowski examined the damage. There was green paint and rust visible in the dent big enough to scrape the tire. Some of the paint was missing. He scraped a bit of the paint into an evidence bag, hoping to match it to the dumpster that was hit.

"Here it is. The man said his name was Simon Jones. He had a funny accent and didn't strike me as a *Simon Jones*. The other guy never said a word, and if I had to guess, I think he was afraid of the other guy."

Harlow took the receipt and read the address. "Markowski, look at this."

Markowski read what Harlow saw. "Shit, that's Faraday's address."

"Mr. Winters, did they happen to give you a deposit for the work?" Harlow asked.

"No, with an address like that, I didn't bother."

"I'm going to ask you for a big favor. Can you call Mr. Jones? Tell him that because the job is not going through his insurance, you need a cash deposit."

"Sure, but he's going to ask why," Winters said.

"Say your wife or partner is giving you grief. Ask for one of them to come in with it and set up a time because you're so busy."

Winters took the receipt back from Markowski and dialed. "Yeah, hello, this is GW Auto Repair. You left your car here for repairs." Winters nodded to Harlow and Markowski and gave them a thumbs-up.

"I need you to come in and give me a deposit. Sorry about that, but because it's not an insurance job, my wife is giving me grief over it."

Winters nodded some more as he listened. "Glad you understand. Yeah, you know how women can be. But, listen, I'm in and out this afternoon. Give me a time, and I'll be here for you."

He nodded again and gave another thumbs-up, "Two hours will work fine. I'll see you then."

Harlow clapped him on the shoulder, "You did great, Mr. Winters."

"What about the other one?" Winters was suddenly worried. "What if you catch the quiet one and the mean one comes looking for him?"

"You let us worry about that," Harlow told him. "Where can we get a cup of coffee around here while we put this together?"

"There's a café on the next block," Winters said.

Driving away from the repair shop, Harlow said, "Call Bradenton PD. Let them know what's going on. They might want to send a car or two to cruise the area in case our suspects show up early."

"On it, boss," Markowski said, punching in numbers.

Chapter Twenty-Six

"Max, I'm worried about what Winters said. We don't know which one will show up. Or maybe they both do, or they could send someone else," Markowski said.

"We can handle it, no matter which way it goes," Harlow said. The server poured two cups of strong, hot coffee and asked if they want to order.

"I'll have a breakfast sandwich with sausage, thanks, sweetie," Harlow answered. He dumped a packet of sugar and two of the little tubs of Half and Half in his coffee.

Markowski dropped the menu and asked for a Belgian waffle.

"You want a side order of sausage or bacon with the waffle?" asked the server.

"No thanks, that will be fine," Markowski said, as she walked away.

Harlow put his coffee down. "I always wondered about that."

"About what?"

"I know you're Jewish...."

"Yeah, I know. I break some of the rules from time to time, like going to the temple maybe once or twice a year when my mother calls and nags me. I don't go around wearing the funny hat," Markowski laughed, "but it's how I grew up. Going to Hebrew school and the whole Bar Mitzvah thing was expected." Markowski shook two packets of sugar into his coffee. "Sometimes, the smell of bacon drives me crazy."

"My ex used to say that sausage and bacon were going to clog my arteries and give me a heart attack. So, she only bought all the turkey bacon, and turkey sausage. It was never the same," Harlow commiserated.

The detectives ate their meals quickly but took their time over coffee. Harlow asked for another cup to help pass the time as he watched the clock ticking away.

Markowski answered a call from the Bradenton PD and explained the situation to Lieutenant Barrington, who would oversee their end. He promised to send a couple of patrol cars around immediately.

"Can we have a couple of your people in the area in plain clothes? We could use one or two in the garage in case things don't go as planned," Markowski said. He was still worried about who might show up.

A few more minutes of the phone, and Markowski hung up. "Bradenton is on board. We better move."

Harlow called the server over and asked for the check, leaving a $5 tip.

They parked two blocks down the road from the repair shop and walked the rest of the way.

Two detectives walked into the garage and knocked on the open office door. Winters was startled, thinking the dealers had shown up early. They found Winters sitting at his desk in his office. He said: "I was hoping you two were coming to the party. I'm getting nervous sitting here watching the clock."

Then the Bradenton officers arrived. The senior of the men introduced themselves. "I'm Officer

Whitley, and my partner is Officer Hendricks from the Bradenton PD."

"Thanks for coming," Harlow said.

"Glad to help. Where do you want us?" Whitley said.

Harlow told Markowski to instruct the officers to act as employees repairing the cars.

When Markowski returned to the office, Harlow told Winters to look busy while waiting for the suspect to show up.

"My partner and I will stay in the office with the door cracked so we can listen to what's happening. When this suspect shows up, you come back here for paperwork for him to sign. That will get you out of harm's way."

"I like the idea of getting out of harm's way," Winters said, relieved but anxious.

They didn't have long to wait. A car pulled into the lot and a young man hurried into the shop.

Seeing the man, Winters called out across the car he was working on. "Hey there. Sorry to make you come all the way again to Bradenton. My wife ripped me a new one when she found out I didn't collect a deposit."

The man handed Winters an envelope with $500 in it. "It's okay. I just need the car fixed. My wife is pissed I wrecked it. Women, hugh? " He shifted nervously, looking around.

The two plainclothes officers left the car they pretended to work on and circled behind the young man to block his escape.

"I'll be a right back with a receipt," Winters said, rushing back to his office and safety.

Harlow cautioned him, "Stay here."

"No problem there, detective."

As soon as the suspect saw the detectives, he

backed up, looking for a way out. He backed up right into the arms of the officers at the shop entrance.

"I didn't want any of this," he said, hanging his head. "I was doing an errand for a friend."

"First, let's have your name," Harlow demanded.

"Misha Kalashnik." Misha had convinced Sergi that Faraday was not going to be able to talk to the police. He was near death and could not help identify either of them. Sergi believed him but made him redeem himself by bringing the deposit to the garage.

"Russian, right?" Harlow pulled another cigar from his pocket and toyed with it. "Lou, have our friend here escorted to Sarasota." Harlow asked Markowski: "I have a lot of questions."

Markowski cuffed Kalashnik and led him to a Sarasota patrol car.

Harlow stopped to thank the Bradenton officers for their help. Lieutenant Barrington walked over. "It was a pleasure working with you, Harlow," he said, shaking the detective's hand. "Let me know what develops on your end and if you'll be needing us again."

"I appreciate the help. I'll keep you informed."

Harlow turned to leave as Markowski marched up beside him, phone in hand. "Boss, we have another body."

Chapter Twenty-Seven

Traffic on the John Ringling Bridge heading west to St. Armands and Longboat Key was at near stand-still. The view from the top of the high bridge stretched from the purple Van Wezel Performing Arts Center to the condos lining the bay. Harlow, siren blaring, lights flashing, cursed at the snowbird vehicles that would not or could not get out of his way fast enough.

He finally made it over the hump to Bird Key Park, where several marked patrol cars, an ambulance, and Murphy were converged.

The park was nestled at the western base of the Ringling Bridge and ran along the bay. It served as a starting point for many of the thousands of walkers and joggers who used the bridge for exercise as well as a picnic area. It sat at a set of traffic lights that announced the entrance to the Bird Key Yacht Club. Harlow could imagine the residents on the gated community with some of the most expensive waterfront mansions in Sarasota complaining about the congestion on their doorstep.

Harlow and Markowski walked over to Murphy, looking over a gaunt male figure laid out on the ambulance gurney.

"What happened to this guy?" Harlow said.

"His friend is over there," Murphy indicated a waif-like girl sitting beside Officer Gleason. "She said he tried to fly off the bridge like a seagull."

"Interesting," Harlow said. He took a cigar out and lit it before going to see what the girl had to offer.

Officer Gleason stood as Harlow approached, wrinkling her nose at the cigar.

"I'm outside," Harlow grumbled, tilting his Panama hat back in mock respect.

As he got closer, he could see that the girl was older than he thought at first. She was maybe in her early thirties. Living on the Florida streets had aged her face. Her body was rail thin as a teenager.

"Sorry about your friend. Tell me about what happened here? Let's start with your name."

"Amanda Jessup. My friend is, *was*, Craig Lester. We come here to hang out sometimes. The cops like to chase us off. Our kind is not wanted around here. Craig said he had a special treat coming his way today. He said it was bath salts, and he wouldn't even have to get wet. He laughed like it was some big joke. I didn't understand it."

Harlow and Markowski looked at each other. Markowski leaned into Harlow and whispered, "It's hitting the streets."

A tear escaped, trailing down her dirty face, leaving a streak, as the ambulance pulled out of the park, followed by Dr. Murphy's van.

"He wasn't a bad kid, just really screwed up. Craig would swallow, inject or inhale anything to get high."

"Who gave him the bath salts today?" Harlow said.

"I'd never seen this man before, and I didn't get introduced." She was getting aggravated with the questions and nervously bouncing on the bench.

"Then what happened?" Harlow said, coaxing her along.

"Craig was given this little packet of powdery crystal stuff. It looked like what my mom used to sprinkle in my bath when I was little. After the man left, Craig poured the whole packet into his mouth. I told him not to, but he never listens to me." More tears streamed down her face. Officer Gleason offered fresh tissue.

"After a few minutes, I noticed he was watching the seagulls flying overhead. Just staring at them, trying to sound like them. It was weird. It was like he had left the planet. Then, all of a sudden, he jumped up and started running up the bridge, screaming like a seagull. When he got to the top, he tore off his shirt, climbed up on the rail, and jumped. I swear he was flapping his arms trying to fly."

"Jesus," Markowski said softly.

"I hope you have him on speed dial 'cause we're going to need him," Harlow answered.

Chapter Twenty-Eight

"Clair, what can you tell me about this guy?" Harlow asked, looking at Craig Lester laid out on the stainless-steel table. Murphy had begun the autopsy. The man's chest was flayed open, revealing his bloody insides. No matter how many of these Harlow had attended, it still grossed him out to see another human body so undignified this way. He didn't want to be reminded about what would happen to him when he died.

Dr. Murphy projected a couple of X-rays up for Harlow to see.

"Our friend here fractured his spine in three places, had a broken arm and multiple abrasions, and impact injuries to his insides."

She pointed out the injuries and turned back to the table. "He might have gotten away with trying to fly. It was like hitting concrete. The tide was out. He hit some of the bridge pilings on the way down and landed on the oyster reefs at low tide."

"Have you run the tox screen yet?" Harlow said.

"It's running now. What's interesting is Mr. Lester wasn't long for this Earth before he took flight. He had severe liver damage, and his kidneys were failing. Look at this."

Murphy moved to the top of the table and gently opened Craig's mouth. "Most of his teeth were rotten or had already fallen out. His nasal cavity is destroyed from sniffing cocaine and whatever else he was into." Moving down to the victim's arms, she showed a trail of needle marks. "Needle marks on both arms. Some healed and some more recent. I bet it was getting hard for him to find a vein to shoot into. He's at least fifty pounds underweight and shows signs of being bitten by bed bugs. This guy was trying to kill himself."

"That pretty much jives with what his friend at the scene said." Harlow stepped away from the table. He stood near the door a moment before turning back and putting his hands in his pockets and rocking on his heels. He was trying to piece it all together.

"You said that this kid didn't have long to live anyway, but it was still a hell of a way to die. We'll need that tox screen. If I find the dealer, can you match the chemical makeup to what Lester took?"

"There are some variables, but yes, we could match it. So long as the recipe is the same, there should not be a problem," Murphy said.

"We've got to get this stuff off the streets. Let me know what you find."

"I will. Max, this runaway drug is not your fault. Dealers are always looking for new ways to push this crap. They don't care about the lives they ruin. All they care about is the money."

Harlow walked over to Murphy. "That's why I like you, Murph. You always make me feel better. Even on a day like this."

Harlow moved closer and almost took her gloved hands in his before he realized where her hands had been.

Murphy yanked off the gore-covered gloves and reached out to the detective.

Harlow acknowledged the gesture and squeezed her hands. "You know how to listen, and you say what I need to hear." Harlow stared deep into her eyes, leaning ever closer.

"Hey, boss, we got to go," Markowski called from the door.

"Shit," Harlow mumbled.

"Another time, Max," Clair said, smiling and blushing.

The doctor watched the detectives as they rushed down the hall. Leaning against the doorframe to the morgue, she rubbed her hands together, remembering how gentle the gruff detective could be.

"Did I interrupt something there between you and Doc?" Markowski asked on the way out of the building.

"I'm not sure," Harlow said. "Maybe. Yet to be decided."

Chapter Twenty-Nine

Misha Kalashnik fidgeted in an interrogation room. Harlow and Markowski watched him through the one-way window.

Kalashnik slumped, head down, picking at his fingernails.

Markowski handed Harlow a folder. "The vehicle at the repair shop belongs to Anya Melnikov. She reported it stolen yesterday morning. She's Russian born. I checked, and she came to this country as a teenager years ago."

"Let's see what this guy has to say," Harlow said, opening the door.

"Mr. Kalashnik, you brought the deposit money to the repair shop today. How did you end up doing that?"

"It was all my stupid brother-in-law's idea. I didn't want to have anything to do with it," Kalashnik said, looking down at his nails which were starting to bleed.

"Your brother-in-law's name?" Harlow said.

"Don't know if I should tell you."

"Well, let me tell you about how many years you are going to spend in jail."

"It was not my fault. Sergi made me do it," he

shouted. He sat back in his chair, crossing his arms across his chest.

"This Sergi is your brother-in-law. I'm willing to bet that his last name is Melnikov. I'm also willing to bet that Anya Melnikov is your sister. How am I doing so far?" Harlow said, looking at his partner. Markowski stood and left the room to run the names through the FBI and Interpol databases.

Kalashnik panicked when he realized what he had revealed. "Sergi is mean. He's going to kill me if he thinks I snitched."

"We can keep you safe if you cooperate with us. Unfortunately, there is more than just stealing and crashing your sister's car. Two people have been murdered. Did you and Sergi Melnikov have anything to do with the murders of Bert Metcalf and Daniel Brookmeyer?"

"I don't think I want to talk anymore. None of what happened was my fault."

Markowski marched in and slapped a folder down in front of him. "It seems that your brother-in-law has quite a record. Sergi Melnikov's got a file cabinet full of arrests for drugs and assault. He's been in a revolving door, in and out of jail since he was a juvenile."

"I still can't snitch. Sergi's mixed up with some dangerous people, real badasses. They'll go after anyone who messes with them."

"We're going to keep you here a while and see if that changes your mind. Talking to us is the only way to stop these people and save yourself," Harlow said.

Markowski opened the door and called in an officer to take the suspect to a cell.

"What are you going to charge him with?" Markowski said.

"For now, just the stolen vehicle. We need more

evidence to charge him with murder," Harlow said. "How about we call the sister in and rattle her cage a bit? Maybe she doesn't know what her husband is up to? If she does, then she can be charged as an accessory to murder."

"I'll get a warrant to search her house. What about Sergi Melnikov?" Markowski said.

"Find him and bring him in."

Chapter Thirty

Harlow walked into the morgue. The antiseptic stench of blood and death greeted him at the door.

Clair Murphy was deep in the viscera of a woman on the slab in front of her. The detective knocked on the stainless-steel counter beside the door.

"Sorry, I didn't want to surprise you," Harlow said, approaching the table reluctantly. "What happened here? Anything I need to know about?"

"I was going to call you. This young person was found in a park in the Rosemary District. A young mother with her two-year-old discovered the body. The victim was on the platform at the top of one of the slides."

"You have a cause of death yet?"

"I had the tox screen expedited. It's the same as Craig Lester, a mix of heroin and meth. We're dealing with another death by bath salts."

"Has she been identified yet?"

"Yes, her name's Jennifer Esposito. Another lost soul living on Sarasota streets. She'd been a long-time drug user with track marks on her arms. In pretty bad shape, health-wise."

"Just like Craig Lester. Shit, how much of this stuff is out there?" Harlow groaned. They had to find the source of the synthetic drug and fast before more bodies landed in Murphy's morgue.

"You have time for lunch today? I'll be finished here in an hour," Murphy asked. Usually, she waited for Harlow to make the first move and ask her. Today, Murphy decided to put on her big girl pants and ask the detective. Busy as she was, if more of this drug hit the streets, they would be even more backed up.

"Sorry. Looks like I'm going to be grabbing something at my desk today. How about a drink after work at Duffy's?" Harlow inched closer to Murphy but backed off when he realized her gloved hands were covered in blood.

"We're getting some leads that might point to the dealer. I want to stay on top of things. Fill you in tonight, if that's okay?"

Harlow looked at Murphy and hesitated. He wanted to say more but couldn't.

"Sorry about lunch, Clair. I would have liked that," Harlow said.

"That's fine. Give me a call and I'll meet you at Duffy's."

Keeping it casual might be the best course, Murphy thought as she turned back to the girl on the table.

Chapter Thirty-One

Anya Melnikov was slumped in Interrogation when Harlow walked back into the station with a Jimmy John's sub and soft drink.

Markowski cornered him before he reached his desk. "Anya Melnikov says she didn't know what her husband and brother were up to. I'm inclined to believe her."

"Get her a coffee or something and have her wait. Where are we on catching Mr. Melnikov ?" Harlow asked, throwing his lunch on his papered desk. He wanted to eat before interviewing Mrs. Melnikov .

"His wife gave us some places he likes to hang out. We're checking them now."

Harlow sat and unwrapped his sub and took a long pull on his drink. "Give me a minute to scarf this down. I don't think I ate anything yesterday. See if she has any idea where he was on the night of Metcalf's murder. As well as the night Daniel Brookmeyer was killed. She must know something."

Harlow joined Markowski after his hurried lunch.

Anya Melnikov was an attractive woman in her late thirties. Harlow noticed that she wore little make-up but didn't need it. Her dress was a light-blue print with a matching scarf wrapped around her dark hair.

"I don't understand why I'm here. I told your

sergeant that I don't meddle in my husband's business," she said, looking Harlow in the eye.

"What exactly is your husband's business?" Harlow said.

"He works for one of those crappy motels down on Tamiami Trail."

Chapter Thirty-Two

After speaking with Anya Melnikov , Detectives Harlow and Markowski wasted no time visiting the motel where Sergi Melnikov was supposed to work. After snaking their way through the afternoon snowbird traffic, they pulled into the parking lot in front of the Seaside Motel.

"I wouldn't let a dog stay here," Harlow groaned, looking at the decrepit building in front of him.

The motel was a leftover from the Florida tourist heyday of the fifties and sixties. The paint was peeling or missing entirely from the old pine wood siding. Rusting air conditioners hung out from the bottom of the cloudy windows. A Vacancy sign with missing letters flashed below a washed-out sign announcing the Seaside Motel free Wi-Fi included, cable tv.

The detectives walked into the small, dark office and tapped the small counter bell. The place reeked of mold and body odor. An unshaven youth of about twenty emerged, wearing a dirty tee-shirt with the sleeves cut off.

He looked the detectives up and down, pushing his unruly brown hair out of his eyes.

"It's fifty dollars for an hour. If you want to stay longer, it's another twenty-five for each extra hour."

The young man stood waiting, scratching his beard with a blank stare.

"Detective Harlow from the Sarasota PD and my partner, Detective Sergeant Markowski," Harlow said, flashing his badge.

The kid instantly turned and took off through the back room, stumbling and crashing into the junk stowed there, running to reach the back door. Markowski rounded the counter, grabbing the kid and tossing him to the grubby tile floor before slapping handcuffs on him.

Markowski dragged him back to the lobby, presenting him to Harlow.

"What's your name, and why did you try to run?" Harlow said.

The young man's eyes had the vacant look of a habitual drug user, but he volunteered: "James Scholfield."

"Right, but why did you run?"

"Don't like cops. You guys are always harassing me for no reason."

Markowski showed Harlow the track marks on the kid's forearms. Then, pulling up the back of his tee-shirt, Markowski discovered an infestation of swollen bedbug bites.

"Same as the two dead overdoses," Harlow said. "Listen up. We're looking for Sergi Melnikov. He's supposed to be the manager here."

Scholfield shuffled his flip-flops, turned his head, and looked away toward the outside traffic. "Never heard of him."

"I don't believe you. Try again," Harlow growled. "You have a choice. Tell me what I want to know or spend some time as our guest downtown. No room service, no cable. I hear it hurts real bad when you need a fix."

Fear crept into Scholfield's bloodshot eyes. The idea of spending time in a cell loosened his tongue. "He's not here. Melnikov said he'd be back in an hour. He had to see someone, said he was owed some money."

"Now, that wasn't so hard, was it?"

"You gonna let me go? I told you what you wanted to know."

Harlow pulled two images from a photo pack and showed them to Scholfield. "Have you ever seen either of these two people before?"

Scholfield stared at the photos of Craig Lester and Jennifer Esposito.

"They're dead?"

"Yes. Do you know them? We believe they might have spent some time here."

"Yeah, they crashed here for a couple days. Craig was into some bad shit. Jennifer was nice. Flirty. She talked to me."

"I suggest you clean up your act, or you'll be joining Craig and Jennifer in the morgue," Harlow said. "Get this kid back to the station. Give him Miranda."

Markowski checked Scholfield's pockets before handing him over to the waiting officers for transport. "Well, well, look what we have here." Markowski held a dozen tiny packages of crystalline powder in his gloved hand. "This look familiar, Max?"

"Same packaging that Craig Lester's friend described. Mr. Scholfield, you and I are going to have a long conversation. Take him away," Harlow told the waiting officers.

"We have to find out who owns this dump," Harlow said to Markowski.

"I'm on it, Max," Markowski said, walking away, already dialing.

"See if you can get a judge to issue a search warrant on this place."

Chapter Thirty-Three

Harlow walked into the antiseptic morgue looking for Dr. Murphy. Checking around, he found her sitting in her office, poring over a stack of papers.

He entered after rapping softly. He placed the packages from Schofield's pockets on top of the papers.

"Guess what we found today?"

"Did you find the dealer?" Murphy said, taking her reading glasses off, and turned to face him with a faint smile.

"Not yet, but we're closer. We arrested someone today, James Scholfield. He had a bunch of these in his pocket."

"How did you find him?"

"Anya Melnikov told us her husband is the manager of a flea motel on Tamiami Trail, the Seaside Motel. Up by Ringling College. The guy working the desk was carrying these."

"I know that place. It looks like a strong wind will blow the whole thing down," Murphy said. "I'll have the lab analyze these and see if it's a match to what Lester took." Murphy put her glasses on to study a packet

."There's something else. Scholfield had a colony of bedbug bites like our other two ODs. So, they might have stayed there at some time."

"Could be," Murphy said. "You still up for that drink tonight? I'm about done here."

"I wish I could. Markowski is trying to find out who owns the Seaside, and we haven't found Melnikov yet. There's surveillance at his house and the motel. He'll turn up, eventually. Misha Kalashnik told us that Melnikov was giving the orders, but who is giving Melnikov orders? We're close," Harlow said. "Anyway, I wanted to drop by. Sorry about skipping a drink tonight. Raincheck?"

"Sure, I understand, Max."

Murphy watched the detective leave her office and sighed. "Oh well. Duffy's is not going anywhere." Picking up her glasses, she chewed on the stem a moment before putting them on. Murphy shuffled through a few pages in front of her before she tore the glasses off, throwing them on the desk. "Shit."

Chapter Thirty-Four

Markowski barged into the squad room. "We got him. They picked up Melnikov. Stupid bastard was at the Seaside all this time. We got Judge Harrison to issue the warrant. Our officers went through all the rooms. A few were empty," Markowski said. "That place is disgusting. You would not believe the shit we found. We arrested three people on drug charges—two more on prostitution. We have them down in Central Booking.

"Melnikov was hiding away in one of the rooms. He was laying there watching cable and scarfing down some Chinese. You should have seen the look on his face. Priceless."

"Good work," Harlow said. "Let's see what this guy has to say."

Melnikov looked up as the detectives marched into the interrogation room. "Why am I here? I have done nothing wrong."

"Mr. Melnikov, we believe you and Misha Kalashnik have killed two people. We also believe that you are involved in dealing a dangerous drug out of that motel. You call that nothing?" Harlow said.

"Again, that had nothing to do with me." Melnikov stared at the detectives. Leaning back in his seat, he said, "I want a lawyer."

"Have it your way," Harlow said, standing. "Take our friend here to his cell and get him a lawyer."

Markowski signaled for an officer.

"I'll be out in an hour," the suspect shouted back at the detectives.

Approaching the detectives, an officer called out, "We found out who owns the motel. Some rich guy out on Lido Key."

"Let's take a ride. It's a beautiful day to check out the beach," Harlow said. He put on his hat and filled his pocket with cigars.

"I hope you're not planning on smoking those smelly things on the way?" Markowski asked. "I just got the stink out from the last time."

Chapter Thirty-Five

Yellow crime scene tape still fluttered in the Gulf breeze at the park near the west end of the Ringling Bridge as the detectives drove past it.

Traffic around St. Armands Circle was bumper to bumper in the late afternoon. The aroma of paella from the Columbia Restaurant and the garlic and thyme of seafood invaded their air-conditioned cruiser. Tanned locals and sunburned tourists stepped into the traffic roundabout as if they owned the island that John Ringling once did. Navigating their way through the snowbirds shopping on the circle took several pre-cious minutes.

The home of Ivan Vassiliev was a grand res-idence surrounded by a six-foot-high wrought iron fence and security gate. Harlow and Markowski spot-ted several surveillance cameras covering the entrance and the manicured grounds that were golf-course perfect.

Markowski pressed the intercom button by the gate. A hollow voice called out, "Vassiliev residence. What is your business?"

Sarasota Police Department. We want to speak to Mr. Vassiliev. Now."

"About what do you want to speak to him?"

"Your motel and your manager, Mr. Melnikov," Markowski told the voice.

The gate slowly swung open. The detectives stopped at the bottom of a staircase leading to the teak front door of a mansion big enough to be a hotel. Giant urns overflowing with exotic flowers guarded the front door.

The door was opened by a tall, well-built man in his early 40s, wearing a loose cotton button-down shirt in a tropical print.

"Mr. Vassiliev is on the patio. Come with me, please," the man said in a heavy Russian accent.

Markowski nudged Harlow and pointed to the gun tucked neatly under the man's shirt as they followed him through the expansive home.

The detectives followed through the home decorated with expensive art and furnishings. Harlow noticed what could be an original Monet over a mantelpiece.

Vassiliev was climbing out of his Olympic-sized infinity pool overlooking Sarasota Bay as the detectives approached. Nude. The Russian dismissed his assistant with a flick of his wrist as he wrapped a towel around his trim waist.

"Gentlemen, I understand you have an interest in that old motel of mine," he said, pouring himself a drink of what looked like vodka. He raised the bottle and a glass, asking, "Would you like some fine Russian vodka? I have it imported especially."

"No, thank you, this is official," Harlow said.

"Please have a seat if we are to discuss business."

Harlow remained standing and jumped right in.

"Mr. Vassiliev, your manager of the Seaside, Sergi Melnikov, is sitting in a cell awaiting a charge of murder along with his brother-in-law Misha Kalashnik.

How long have you owned the motel?"

Vassiliev raised his glass and looked at the cloudless Sarasota sky. "I received that derelict establishment as payment for a debt. It is worthless and of no consequence."

"If it's so worthless, why not sell it?" Harlow asked.

"I use it as a tax write-off. My accountant can help you with that. I assure you it is all legal."

"Did you know your manager allows prostitutes to use the motel? We think drugs are also peddled from there."

"I assure you I know nothing of these things. I've never even been there. I am a legitimate businessman. I'm sorry, detective, but I have tickets for the Sarasota Opera." Vassiliev stood, swallowed the last of the vodka, and signaled his gun-toting assistant. "Victor, please show these detectives out."

"That's okay, Vic. We can find our way," Markowski said.

Chapter Thirty-Six

"What do you think of Vassiliev?" Harlow asked his partner, driving back to the station, crossing back over the Ringling Bridge.

Looking out the windshield at a large yacht passing underneath, Markowski shook his head. "Lucky bastard."

"Who, Vassiliev?"

"No, that yacht down there. How do people afford toys like that? He's throwing enough wake to surf behind. What do those young girls see in these old geezers, anyway?"

"Coast Guard will have something to say about how fast he's going in this waterway by the bridge. That boat cost more than I'll ever see in my lifetime. Vassiliev seems to do alright for himself. Get someone to check him out. A businessman? What business? I don't trust him." Harlow merged into the lane for the turn onto Fruitville Road.

"I have an idea he's knee-deep in this drug business. He owns the motel where Sergi runs a whorehouse. Two drug overdoses caused by bath salts could be connected. That's big money. Anya Melnikov's brother is involved in the murder of Bert Metcalf and Daniel Brookmeyer. All roads lead back to Vassiliev."

"That so-called assistant of his, Victor, was packing heat. I wonder how he fits into all this? And what's with all the security?" Markowski was interrupted by a call. Hanging up, he said, "That was Wilson. Mrs. Metcalf is waiting for us at headquarters."

Chapter Thirty-Seven

"Mrs. Metcalf, I'm surprised to see you here. What can I do for you?" Harlow asked, taking a seat at his desk.

"Have you found out who murdered my husband?" The new widow sat in a dark navy dress. Dark circles underlined her red-rimmed eyes from crying.

"There have been some recent developments we are looking into. We hope we will have some answers soon."

"That is good to hear. I was afraid that no one was interested in solving Bert's murder because he's not some rich Sarasota retiree."

"Not at all, Mrs. Metcalf. Is there anything else I can do for you?"

"Yes, that's really why I came. I was thinking about that phone call Bert got about Mr. Smith and the chair. When he hung up and came back to the table, he said, 'What a strange accent. Russian maybe?'"

"Mrs. Metcalf, you remembered it now, and that's the important thing." Harlow stood and reached across the desk to shake her hand.

"Are you sure the man's name was Romanoff?"

"Yes, I remembered it because it's the name of the Russian royal family who was killed during the

Revolution. I thought it odd at the time."

"That could be just a coincidence. Please, if you remember anything else, get in touch with me."

Dr. Murphy rapped on the door and let herself in. "Mrs. Metcalf, how are you doing?"

"Things are going well. I'm changing things at the shop, carrying more upmarket items and collectibles, and finally seeing a small profit again. Bert loved garage sales and found most of the stuff for the shop that way. No one wanted to buy that junk. Poor man, he tried so hard."

Standing beside Harlow, Murphy asked, "How is your son? You were very worried about him."

"He's doing well. Chris is pulling his grades up and looking into courses at the Sarasota Tech. He's even been teaching me how to use the computer for business. Excel. Google Sheets and stuff."

"I'm glad for both of you."

"I must be going. It was nice seeing you both again." Mrs. Metcalf picked up her handbag and left.

"I missed some of that. What did she have to say?" Murphy asked, taking the seat that Mrs. Metcalf had vacated.

"She said the call her husband received about the chair was a man with a Russian accent. Heavy. This case seems to circle like a Sarasota roundabout loaded with Russians. All we need is to have the Russian mob make Sarasota home for their drug dealing. I also think Misha Kalashnik knows more than he's telling us. I want to talk with him again."

Clair tossed a folder at Harlow. "I think you'll find this interesting reading. The drug that killed our two OD victims is a chemical match for the drugs you found on Melnikov . So, that looks like a connection to him and the Seaside Motel."

"Melnikov has lawyered up. We'll have to

question him with his lawyer present. We won't get much out of him."

Harlow stood and paced around the room. "I have to talk with Vassiliev again too. I can't get over the feeling that he is involved in this. He's slippery as an Everglades eel. And that assistant of his, Victor, is more of a bodyguard than an assistant."

"Why don't you let me cook you something tonight for supper, something simple? You have to eat, and we can talk about the case, if you want to or not." Clair knew how much it was bothering Max and worried he would burn himself out over it. She found that she was caring for the gruff detective. Was he ready for a relationship again? Was she?

Chapter Thirty-Eight

Misha Kalashnik sat in the interrogation room, playing with his fingernails again. Three of his fingers were bandaged to keep him from damaging them further. Still, he picked at the medical tape. He needed a cigarette. His nerves were at the breaking point. He jumped as detectives Harlow and Markowski marched in.

"Look, we know you have more to tell us about who is at the heart of this operation. If you talk to us now, it will go a long way to helping you. Start talking. Save yourself. We know you're afraid of someone. We can protect you," Harlow said.

"Sergi is bad news, but the people he works for are worse."

"What work does he do for these people? Drugs?" Harlow asked. He pretty much already knew what work it was, but he needed to hear the admission from Misha.

"Drugs. Sergi cooks meth and coke for drug dealers. Big time. He said if I told Anya, he'd hurt her and me. Oh God, he's going to kill me." He put his head in his handcuffed hands and sobbed.

Harlow circled the table and put his hand on Kalashnik's shoulder. "Sergi Melnikov is in our custody. He's not going anywhere if I can help it. He's chilling downstairs in one of our comfy guest cells."

A knock on the door. Everyone looked up. Officer Wilson called Markowski over and whispered. Turning back to Harlow, he said, "Sergi made bail. He's out."

"Shit, how the hell did he do that?" Harlow shouted.

"I told you. He'll come after me and kill me. You can't protect me," Kalashnik cried, jumping up and running his bandaged hands through his greasy hair.

"Wilson said that some smart-ass lawyer in a sharkskin suit showed up and posted his bail," Markowski said.

"That one fucking phone call. Sergi called who-ever he worked for, and they sent the shyster lawyer," Harlow said. He turned to the suspect. "If you don't start talking, you're going down for all of it. You are going to take the rap for killing Bert Metcalf and Daniel Brookmeyer. Kidnapping Arthur Faraday alone gets you twenty-five to life. You talk to us, and maybe we can keep you from getting the electric chair up in Starke. Or do you want the needle? Who does Melnikov work for?" Harlow yelled.

"He works for some rich dude on Lido Key. I went there with him once. He talked with this big scary guy he called Victor."

Chapter Thirty-Nine

"You thinking the same thing I am?" Harlow asked
Markowski as they hustled out to the parking lot
across from Payne Park.

"Yeah, we need to revisit Vassiliev. I wish we
could get Melnikov to open up and talk," Markowski
said, starting the engine.

They drove back out to Lido Key, stopping in
front of the iron gates protecting Vassiliev's mansion.

Markowski pressed the call button on the intercom and waited.

"How much do you figure this dump is worth?
I saw in the paper some big-ass mansion sold for $12
million last weekend," the younger detective wondered
out loud.

"We'd need to hit the lottery big time to afford a
palace like this," Harlow replied.

"May I help you," a voice they recognized now
as Victor.

"Detectives Harlow and Markowski to see Mr.
Vassiliev."

"Mr. Vassiliev has already answered all your
questions."

Harlow was frustrated with being dismissed.
"We have more questions for your boss. If we have

to, we can come back with a search warrant. Probably make a mess. A big-ass mess."

The gate slowly rattled open. Once again, they parked in front of the massive home. Harlow was fed up and slammed his door. Suddenly, the sprinklers ignited. They dodged a heavy burst of gray, untreated irrigation water. Was this mogul sending them a message?

"When we get back to the station, I want everything you can find out on this guy's finances. How the hell does he afford this place?" Harlow said, shaking droplets from his hat.

Victor was waiting at the door to take the detectives to Vassiliev. Victor guided them through to an office where Vassiliev was sitting behind an antique mahogany desk. The walls were lined with bookcases filled with leather-bound classics in English, French, and Russian. The room was decorated with art and expensive-looking objects. A Lalique vase graced a dainty polished table.

Watching Harlow, Vassiliev said, "You appreciate my artwork?"

"Yes, this an original Monet?" Harlow asked. He pointed to a painting titled *Sunrise* on the wall over a sideboard holding delicate crystal decanters filled with liquor.

"I'm impressed, detective. It's not as well-known as some of his other works, but I liked that it showed a sailboat. So appropriate for Sarasota, don't you think?"

"I appreciate nice things. Even ones I know I can't afford."

Vassiliev looked hard at the detective and realized that Harlow was someone he would have to be very careful around. The Russian poured chilled vodka into crystal glass from a matching crystal decanter. He lifted his glass, offering the detectives a drink. They declined.

"Why are you gentlemen back? I answered your questions, and I assure you I have nothing to do with that Seaside Motel. Yes, I own the property, but I do not know what goes on there."

"We believe you do know. Do you know what a cook is? And not the restaurant kind. Your manager, Sergi Melnikov, is cooking drugs at your motel. He is also dealing drugs there. People are dying. The place is disgusting."

Harlow could tell that Vassiliev knew what Melnikov was doing at the motel.

Vassiliev poured another vodka. "As I said before, I know nothing about all this. I'm getting tired of these questions and accusations. It's police harassment, and if this continues, I will contact my lawyers." Standing to face the detectives, Vassiliev called out. "Victor, please see these gentlemen out."

Chapter Forty

Markowski pointed to his computer screen. "Max, look at this. I pulled Vassiliev's financial statements. He has a numbered account in the Caymans. We expected that. What's interesting is his local stuff."

Harlow took the pages that spewed from the printer and spread them out over his littered desk. After studying them for a few minutes, he looked up at Markowski.

"This is crazy. Vassiliev has money from the Seaside being deposited into a Sarasota bank. This statement shows twenty grand a month to Melnikov. How many motel managers make that on the North Trail? That's a lot more than a sleazy motel manager should be getting. Why's he getting paid that much?"

"That's pretty standard for a man like him to have offshore accounts, but what's with the local bank?"

Harlow sat back in his squeaky chair. He studied the bank statement. "It's the taxes. If the motel can show a loss every year, he can deduct that on his taxes. Vassiliev pays the utilities, cable, Wi-Fi, insurance, and county tax from this local account. He's a clever bastard."

Markowski stood to think about things for a

moment. "Okay, but how can he afford to live in that big-ass McMansion with all that art and stuff? He told us he was a businessman. Where is he getting his money? Is he one of those oil guys? Shipping? Connections to the Kremlin? Tech inventor? Real estate gambler? Or dealing in sex workers? What do you think?"

"That, my friend, is what we have to find out. I have a theory, but I have to prove it."

Officer Wilson rapped on the door, "You got a problem. Sergi Melnikov was just found dead in Centennial Park."

"Shit," Harlow grabbed his hat and stuffed his pocket with cigars.

Racing out of the building, the detectives jumped into their vehicle and sped north.

The park was nestled on the bay side of Tamiami Trail and a popular boat launching spot. The grand purple building that housed the Van Wezel Performing Arts Center loomed to the south. The whole area was slated to be renovated into a $250 million arts and waterfront recreation park over the next fifteen years.

Harlow had seen many changes over the years, and not all of them were good. Unfortunately, the Sarasota Lawn Bowling Club was not included in the renovation plans. The Bowlers Club occupied the same spot for over one hundred years. Harlow remembered when he and his wife had taken their children to the park when they were little, stopping to watch the matches on a sunny day with the breezes drifting off the bay, ruffling the palm trees, and mangroves.

The sound of traffic negotiating the new round-about disturbed that memory and jolted him back to the present. Following the flashing blue and red lights of the first responders and the police, Harlow and Markowski found Dr. Murphy already on the scene.

"We meet again. What up this time, Murph?"

"Looks like he drowned, except for the bullet hole in the back of his head. A couple walking their dog spotted him in the water under the small fishing pier over there."

"Any idea time of death?"

"Hard to tell since he was in the water. I'd guess sometime after midnight. I'll know better when I get him back to the morgue."

Harlow stood there rocking on his heels and rolling an unlit cigar around in his mouth. Was it just a coincidence that Melnikov was killed shortly after they spoke with Vassiliev?

Chapter Forty-One

"Talk to me, Murphy," Harlow called. He marched into the morgue after trying to do some paperwork at his desk and could not concentrate. His mind kept going around in circles and coming back to Vassiliev and the motel.

He cringed when he saw Melnikov's open skull and the coroner holding a bloody ball of white and gray matter that was his brain.

"Yuck, you really enjoy doing this stuff?"

"Yes, I do. I've been doing this job for thirty years, and it still amazes me the things that one human can inflict on another."

"And I thought I was cynical."

"Look at at this," Murphy said, pointing to a bullet hole in the victim's brain. "It's a .38 caliber. I was surprised the bullet went straight through. No powder burns, so he was not shot at close range. The good thing for us is that if you find the weapon, we have something to match it to."

Moving away from the table, Max Harlow paced the cramped lab. He took a cigar out, sniffed it as if to inhale something other than lab antiseptic before replacing it in his pocket.

"Murphy, if you remember the scene and where

the body was found, I think Melnikov was standing on the seawall looking out over the bay, waiting to meet someone. That someone could shoot him while they were still in the parking lot. Melnikov falls into the water, and the current takes him under the pier."

"I'd go along with that. One more thing." Murphy set the brain down and moved back to the victim. "His lungs were a mess as well as his whole respiratory system. You can see how bloodshot and red his eyes are." Murphy eased open the victim's eyelids. "He probably had pounding headaches, too. Cooking meth was slowly killing him, and the bullet finished him off."

"Murphy, you are a genius. I believed he was cooking meth at the Seaside Motel and mixing it with heroin to make bath salts. Now we have evidence. Too bad they killed him before we could get him to tell us who heads this operation. He lawyered up, and we couldn't get anything out of him."

Murphy tore off her gloves and threw them in the biohazard bin. "I thought you had him in jail. Who bailed him out?"

"I'm checking the paperwork. Whoever bailed Melnikov out set him up to be murdered."

Chapter Forty-Two

Harlow's phone sounded as he was leaving the morgue. Markowski had tracked down the bondsman who bailed Melnikov out.

He picked up his partner at the station, and they drove down Washington Boulevard to a pawn shop that doubled as a bail bond mill.

The owner, a tall, muscular Black man with gray, short hair and beard to match, stood tensely behind the counter. The place was dark and dingy. The walls were lined with discards from people who had no choice but to pawn for money. It smelled like sweat and the failure of hundreds of lives who came here as a last resort.

"What can I do for you, officers?"

Harlow and Markowski looked at each other. The owner was no stranger to the police if he could spot cops that fast.

"Detective Max Harlow and my partner Detective Markowski." The detectives flashed their badges.

The man nodded several times, rolling his tongue around his mouth, thinking. "Jerry Houston. This is my shop. I don't take in any stolen goods if I can help it. People are not always forthcoming about where they got the stuff from."

"We're not interested in the pawn side of your business, but in an alleged felon. You bailed him out of the Sarasota Jail. His name was Sergi Melnikov."

"You said *was*. Am I to assume that Melnikov is dead?"

"He was found shot to death in Centennial Park. We want to know who paid his bail," Harlow said.

"Let me pull it up." Houston disappeared into the back office. Harlow could hear the keyboard keys clicking. Markowski wandered around.

Houston returned with a printout of the bail details for Sergi Melnikov .

Harlow took the paper and called Markowski over. "You seeing the name on this?"

"Yeah, Victor Lenkov. I wonder if it's the same Victor who works for Alexie Vassiliev."

"We need to pay a visit to Victor Lenkov and see why he paid ten percent of five hundred thousand dollars to bail out Melnikov."

Chapter Forty-Three

After entering the mansion on Lido Key, the following day, Detectives Harlow and Markowski were met at the door by an arrogant and unwelcoming Victor Lenkov.

"Gentlemen, Mr. Vassiliev is by the pool finishing his breakfast." Victor turned and expected the detectives to follow.

"Mr. Lenkov, we are here to see you. There are some questions we need answers to," Harlow called to the man's back.

Lenkov stopped and turned around slowly. "What is it you want to know?" Lenkov sneered, stuffed his hands in his pockets, and lifted his chin.

"Why did you bail Sergi Melnikov out of jail?" Harlow asked.

"Where did you get the money from? That's a big pile of cash," Markowski added.

"So many questions. Please have a seat." Lenkov pointed to leather upholstered chairs in a seating area off the hallway. "I will have to inform Mr. Vassiliev that I will be detained."

While waiting for his return, Markowski sat, and Harlow paced the room. It was furnished with two sofas and several upholstered chairs arranged for conversation. A teak buffet set up for serving drinks occupied a space along one wall. A grand marble fireplace graced the opposite wall. Harlow wondered again how Vassiliev could afford the oversized McMansion.

Lenkov returned with Vassiliev beside him. "I understand you have questions for Victor about Sergi Melnikov," Vassiliev said, draping himself gracefully on one of the sofas, exposing a bare thigh. The man really needed to start wearing clothes. He carried an air of superiority that made Harlow want to throttle him.

"Yes, Victor paid Melnikov 's bail. Why? Shortly after he was released from jail, he was killed. Why?"

Lenkov rose and helped himself to a small bottle of orange juice from a fridge behind the bar. "Melnikov worked for me as a manager of my motel. I was helping an employee out. He was a decent manager, not good, but needed."

"The question remains: Who killed him and why?"

"I really can't answer that." Vassiliev returned to the sofa. "I'm sorry Melnikov was killed. He was an employee and nothing more."

"I have another question for you. What kind of business are you in? We checked you out and your financials. There doesn't seem to be any money coming in to support your lifestyle. How do you explain that?"

Vassiliev was visibly shaken by what Harlow said. His glass of orange juice spilled a bit as he tried to drink but then tried to hide it. "I owned an import/export company that did very well. I sold it, and I'm able to live quite comfortably."

Harlow knew that Vassiliev was not telling the whole truth. The company was most likely a front for his drug operation. Whether he sold it or not was up for debate, but his money had to come from somewhere. You don't stow millions in an offshore account for no reason. He thought of Al Capone and how he was finally caught on tax evasion. Maybe digging deeper into Vassiliev's money trail was the way to bring this drug operation crashing down. Then again, Vassiliev was a clever bastard.

"If that's all, detective, I'll have Victor show you out. If this harassment continues, I'll get my lawyer involved," Vassiliev said.

"It's not harassment, Mr. Vassiliev. You'll know it when I'm harassing you. I'll be putting you in handcuffs."

Chapter Forty-Four

Harlow tried to catch up on some paperwork but found it hard to concentrate. His mind was in overdrive, trying to get a handle on this new drug. He knew in his gut that Vassiliev and the Seaside Motel were at the heart of it. Markowski was a valued partner, but he wanted to talk with Clair Murphy. She knew how to listen.

He walked into her office. She wasn't there. Next, he tried the morgue. One of her assistants was cleaning up after an autopsy.

"Hi Jeff, you know where Dr. Murphy is?"

"She's in court today. They'll break for lunch soon. Maybe you can catch here."

Harlow waved thanks, then hurried back to downtown Sarasota and the courthouse. Flashing his badge to get through the checkpoint, he huffed up the stairs as Murphy emerged from the courtroom. She had given evidence on a hit-and-run that killed two people.

"Hey there. What brings you here?" Murphy asked.

"I was hoping to catch you for some lunch."

"Let's just go to the cafeteria here. I don't want to waste time parking and waiting to be served someplace."

"Good idea." Max guided Clair to the elevator and the cafeteria on the next floor.

"So, what made you come looking for me today?" she asked, carrying her tray on the table. She placed her tuna sandwich and iced tea down, taking a sip of her cold drink. "I needed that."

"Markowski and I went to talk with Victor Lenkov. He's the one who bailed out Sergi Melnikov."

"Right, Melnikov's on my table now. I'll get to him as soon as this court thing is finished."

"I believe Lenkov killed him, but Vassiliev gave the order. I just have to prove it."

"If you can find the weapon that might have killed him, I can try to match it to the bullet I dig out of Melnikov," Murphy said. She continued to eat her sandwich. His mind seemed to be a thousand miles away. Putting her sandwich down, she reached out to Harlow, "What's bothering you, Max?"

Harlow was frustrated, and his tone showed it. "I don't have the proof to bring Lenkov in for questioning. I know he did it, but I don't have any proof."

"Can't you get Kalashnik to give you more infor-mation on the drug operation?"

"Kalashnik doesn't know all that much past what Melnikov told him. I need to find out where they are cooking up that drug."

"Have you pressed Anya Melnikov more about her husband? She must know. He was looking sick from cooking the drugs. You can't tell me she didn't notice and wonder."

Harlow shook his head. "I didn't think of that. My wife always knew when I was coming down with something." He pushed his empty plate away and finished his drink. He had more questions for Anya Melnikov. Murphy was right. Anya Melnikov had to know something was wrong with her husband. You don't have all the symptoms Murphy found, and no one notices. That is unless she looked the other way on purpose. Harlow wondered if the wife was more involved than she let on. Maybe she had something to gain if he popped off.

"Thanks, Clair. I need to pursue that idea a little."

Murphy pushed her half-eaten sandwich to the side. During a trial, she lost her appetite. "Glad I could help."

Harlow hesitated, playing with his empty glass. "I was wondering if you might like to see my kids' soccer games on Saturday. They're playing in Lakewood Ranch. I haven't spent much time with them lately, and they've been bugging me to go to one of their games."

Murphy surprised him. "Sure, I used to play soccer back in the day. It'd be fun to watch your kids. They must be getting pretty big by now."

"They are. Johnathan is twelve, and Jana is ten. They're doing well in school and seem to be dealing with the divorce pretty well."

"Good, I'll even spring for lunch after. I can pick you up or meet you there. Let me know what works for you."

Clair looked at her watch. "Got to get back. I'm a witness for the prosecution."

Harlow watched her leave. *What the hell am I doing? Am I ready for this?* Thoughts swirled in his head as he played with his straw and finished his drink.

How far do I want to take whatever it is with Murphy? Am I too old to start a relationship? Can I bring down the drug dealers plaguing this city? Am I capable of making that last big bust before retirement?

Taking his trash to the bin, he mumbled to himself, "All this thinking is giving me a headache."

Chapter Forty-Five

"Mrs. Melnikov , thanks for coming in again. We have a couple more questions," Harlow said, throwing some photos down on the table in front of her.

Markowski started the tape recorder, stating the date, time and who they were interviewing.

The detective noticed how she looked away from the pictures of her dead husband. She inhaled a noisy breath and bit her lip. A worried expression crossed her face before she tried to compose herself.

"I wasn't given any choice. Your storm troopers came to get me. I'm trying to plan my husband's funeral," she replied, spitting venom.

"Sorry you were inconvenienced. Tell me, how was your husband feeling when you last saw him? The medical examiner found several indicators that he was cooking meth. That meth was mixed with heroin to create a drug called Flakka. Its street name is bath salts."

Mrs. Melnikov shrugged. "The man did not have a healthy lifestyle."

"That drug is already responsible for two deaths. There'll be more if we don't get it off the street."

"I told you before. I don't know what my husband was doing besides managing that fleabag motel." She refused to look Harlow in the eyes. She tapped her

117

fingers and played with the strap on her handbag.

"Mrs. Melnikov, if you knew your husband was cooking meth, you can be charged as an accessory on the drug charges at the very least." He paused. She finally looked him in the eyes. "And if you had anything to do with his murder, that's accessory to murder. Do you know Victor Lenkov?"

Mrs. Melnikov looked up, surprised.

"He's the man we suspect of killing your husband. He works for a man named Vassiliev out on the key."

The woman was still twisting the purse strap, her knuckles white with the pressure. "Victor stopped by the motel a couple times. Vassiliev owns it, so it is to be expected."

Harlow sensed he was getting to her. "Mrs. Melnikov, these guys don't play nice. They killed your husband because he screwed up. You could be next."

"I can't tell you anything." A tear escaped down her cheek.

"Tell me where he was cooking. I know you know. We'll charge you with conspiracy in the making of meth. You knew what your husband was doing. You also knew they were dealing drugs out of the Seaside Motel." Harlow hoped to bluff her into talking.

"I can't. They'll kill me. Like they killed Sergi."

"We can protect you. Tell us what you know, and we'll keep you safe."

Markowski shoved a yellow legal pad and pen towards her. "We need you to give us a statement about what you know. Write it all down. We can set you up in a safe house until we put these men behind bars."

She thought this over for a moment; eventually, she took up the pen and pulled the pad close, wiping her eyes with the back of her hand. "If I do this, you promise to keep me safe? I don't want to end up like my husband."

"Yes, this is the only way to put Lenkov and Vassiliev away for a very long time," Harlow told her. He hoped he wasn't lying.

Chapter Forty-Six

Armed with what Anya Melnikov had told them, Harlow and Markowski weaved through downtown Sarasota to an industrial estate on Whitfield Ave. Following close behind were a couple patrol cars and a hazmat unit.

Without sirens to alert anyone inside, the police surrounded the building. Fifteen officers emerged from a half-dozen units in marked and unmarked vehicles surrounding the perimeter. A helicopter circled just out of eyesight. SWAT took the lead.

Harlow and Markowski pulled up in front of unit 125. Cautiously approaching the door, the detectives could smell the chemicals inside. The sound of voices signaled someone was cooking. Now was the chance to stop this dangerous drug from killing more people.

With everyone wearing breathing masks, Harlow signaled to breach the door. Two SWAT officers outfitted in helmets and vests battered the door with a ram.

Harlow counted down, 3,2,1. A loud bang and the door crashed into the warehouse. The team piled into the building, surprising the occupants.

"Police, everyone, stay where you are," Harlow

shouted. Even through the masks, the stench of the chemicals was overpowering. The risk of an explosion made them cautious. A quick look around the room showed a table covered with chemicals and meth cooking away. The room was claustrophobic, and he was thankful to be wearing his mask.

The cook stood where he was too startled and afraid to move. Another man took off like a rabbit out a rear door. Harlow recognized him: Victor Lenkov. The detective smiled.

"I've got you now, you bastard," Harlow muttered.

While officers and the hazmat team secured the suspect and the chemicals, Harlow and Markowski chased Lenkov.

Reaching the parking lot at the back of the building, Harlow saw SWAT officers in a standoff with Lenkov.

"Lenkov, give it up. Put down your gun," Harlow shouted.

Lenkov stood in the middle of the parking lot, surrounded by about twenty police and SWAT officers with guns pointed at him.

"You don't have any way out of this. Put the gun down on the ground, and let's talk." Harlow didn't want to risk Lenkov getting shot. He needed him to bring down Vassiliev.

Lenkov looked to the sky, watching his freedom fly away like the egrets flying overhead, extending his hands, carefully laid down his gun.

-

Chapter Forty-Seven

"Ballistics have matched a slug from your gun to the one that killed Melnikov," Harlow told Lenkov.

Markowski tossed the report on the interrogation room table.

"You killed him because he was a liability. Vassiliev ordered you to kill his meth cook," Harlow said.

Lenkov stared at the scarred and dented table. His hands were in cuffs that chaffed his wrists.

"Melnikov was replaced with James Scholfield. We met Scholfield at the Seaside Motel where he was working the desk. Your boss is Mr. Vassiliev. He is the one who ordered the hit on Melnikov . You were stupid enough to carry it out."

Lenkov bristled at being called stupid. "I did as I was told. My boss, he has treated me well. I owed him."

"Well, unless you help us put Vassiliev away, you get the death penalty. Help us, and it could be twenty-five to life instead."

Markowski answered a call and left the room. He returned a few minutes later and whispered something to Harlow. This frightened Lenkov. He broke out in a sweat.

Harlow waited, stringing out the silence, pulling

a cigar out, running it under his nose. "I'm not supposed to smoke these. Bad for the health and all that, but I smoke to celebrate when I put a bad guy behind bars. It looks like I'll get a chance to light this one up soon. Maybe top it off with a nice whisky."

Lenkov weighed his options, hanging his head in resignation. He could be signing his death warrant either by getting shivved in jail, the electric chair, or even before he got that far. Vassiliev had a long reach.

"What do you want to know?" Lenkov said.

Markowski and Harlow looked at each other. Their deception worked. An officer had made the call so Markowski could make Lenkov think they had more on him.

"Let's start with Vassiliev. Is he the person responsible for putting the bath salts on the street? Did he use the Seaside Motel as a front for his drug business?" Harlow was already sure he knew the answers. "Remember, this interview is being recorded."

"Yes. Vassiliev needed a front to launder money and to run under the DEA radar. He found Melnikov to cook the meth and make the bath salts."

"Where do Misha Kalashnik and Anya Melnikov fit into all this?"

"You know that Misha is Anya's brother? Anya came to the motel one day to see Sergi. We got to talking, and I liked her a lot. She didn't deserve a moron like him. I started to see her sometimes."

"Is that why you murdered Melnikov? Or did Vassiliev order the hit?"

"Both. After the screw-up with the chair, Vassiliev didn't trust him. Misha was already locked up and he didn't know all that much. He just did whatever Sergi told him to do."

"That is one thing that has bothered me from the beginning. Why put the drugs in the chair?"

Lenkov chuckled. "That was Melnikov's idea. We knew that the DEA boys were watching Vassiliev's house and anyone who came or went from there. He thought the Feds would not think anything about a chair being delivered. Melnikov left the chair at the consignment shop, and I was supposed to pick it up. It all went wrong."

Harlow took a loud breath. He needed time to think. "We'll be back. I'll send in some coffee and a sandwich. On the house."

Markowski and Harlow huddled in the squad room.

"How are we going to bring in Vassiliev? He's a pretty slippery character and covered his tracks?" Markowski said. "If we don't do this right, he'll only move down the road and start up all over again."

"Will Lenkov wear a wire and get Vassiliev to give us the ammunition we need?" Harlow wondered out loud to Markowski while playing with his cigar. The idea might work. If not, they'd have to catch Vassiliev red-handed. An idea came to him out of the blue.

"I want to try something. Let's see Lenkov again."

Chapter Forty-Eight

Lenkov looked up from his ham sandwich when the detectives marched in again. He was worried, and the torn-up paper napkin he was playing with showed it. He hadn't asked for a lawyer and knew it would only delay the inevitable. Going to prison was in his future. He must negotiate a deal on his own to avoid the death sentence.

Harlow and Markowski sat across from Lenkov. A knock on the door stopped them. An officer opened the door. "Mr. Lenkov's lawyer is here."

Lenkov was startled. "I didn't ask for a lawyer."

"I'm Josh Rabinowitz. Mr. Vassiliev retained me as your attorney to protect your interest," the lawyer said, handing his cards to Harlow and Lenkov.

"More likely protecting his own interest," Harlow said.

"May I speak with my client, detectives?"

Harlow and Markowski had no choice but to leave the room.

The situation had suddenly gotten more complicated.

A bail hearing was scheduled for the morning. Lenkov had not asked about bail. Anything could happen if he were released on bail, and Lenkov knew that

Vassiliev would not let him live because he didn't trust anyone to keep their mouth shut. Being paranoid had kept Vassiliev out of jail for years. So far.

The detectives waited while Rabinowitz and Lenkov talked. Loud voices came from the interrogation room.

Harlow could tell that Lenkov was terrified of being out on bail where Vassiliev could reach him.

The smarmy lawyer Vassiliev had sent was dressed in an expensive Brooks Brothers suit. Harlow guessed he could see his reflection in the lawyer's polished shoes. The briefcase alone that the man carried was more than a week's pay for a Sarasota detective.

Harlow stood by his desk, rocking on his heels, rolling an unlit cigar around in his mouth. What other underhanded deeds had the lawyer done for Vassiliev? Maybe having a lawyer was not a bad thing. If Rabinowitz got Lenkov out on bail, could Harlow convince Lenkov to cooperate with the police?

Chapter Forty-Nine

The judge set the bail at one million dollars. Rabinowitz argued that the bond was excessive. "My client is not a flight risk. He has a well-paying position with a prominent employer here. Mr. Lenkov would not want to risk losing that. He has no arrest record. There is no reason for such a high bond."

Judge Carmichael disagreed. "Mr. Lenkov is charged with murder, a capital offense. The bail remains at one million, and he will surrender his passport. I want Mr. Lenkov where we can reach him."

Rabinowitz shoved his paperwork into his briefcase went to arrange payment. He left the courtroom in a hurry to report back to Vassiliev.

Once back on the street, Harlow would not be able to talk to Lenkov if he didn't try now. He asked Markowski to delay letting Lenkov leave with Rabinowitz.

"Mr. Lenkov," Harlow said. The man was signing his release papers and collecting his personal items.

"You do know what's going to happen to you as soon as you get out of here? Vassiliev is going to make sure you don't talk to us again."

"I can deal with Vassiliev. I've worked for him for years."

"That's bull, and you know it," Harlow said. He leaned closer to Lenkov, looking around for his lawyer or whoever else might be listening. You know you are going to be convicted of murder. Work with us, and I'll have a word to help you get a lighter sentence." Harlow could tell Lenkov was listening closely.

"What do you want me to do? I'm not saying I'll do it."

"You have to convince Vassiliev that it's in his best interest to keep you alive. Make him think you still want to work for him.

You are indispensable. A loyal employee. As soon as you can, call me."

Harlow handed Lenkov his card. Rabinowitz and Markowski approached them.

Rabinowitz grabbed Lenkov by the arm, pulling him away, "Come on, let's go."

Lenkov hollered back at the detectives, "I'm not talking to you damn cops. I don't care what you threaten me with."

Was Lenkov trying to stay alive? Or just trying to deflect suspicion? And help bring Vassiliev down? Harlow didn't know.

Chapter Fifty

Murphy jumped and yelled when Harlow's son, Johnathan, kicked a field goal right as the whistle for halftime blew.

Sitting on the sidelines, Harlow laughed at how animated Murphy was. She was glowing in the spring heat, but it was more than that. He had never seen her enjoying herself like she was today.

"Did you see that, Max? The kid's a natural. He's what, twelve? If he keeps playing like he is, he could get a college scholarship for soccer. There are several good colleges with soccer programs," Clair said. She grabbed a cold bottle of water from her small cooler pack.

Max took a long drink. "Glad you're enjoying the game. I haven't seen Johnathan play in a long time."

Johnathan came over and stood in front of his father. "Did you see that goal, Dad?" The boy was tall and lanky, perfect for running up and down a soccer field. He would grow up to be a handsome young man.

"I did. Would you like water? You worked hard out there today," Harlow said.

"No, thanks, I have one already." He was awkward in front of his father and Murphy. He shifted from foot to foot, juggling a soccer ball.

"I'm amazed at how good you are. You have a

good team there. How's your coach?"

"Mr. Maddox is great. He used to be on a professional team. He said I might go pro."

"That's great. I'd like you to meet a friend of mine, Dr. Clair Murphy. We work together sometimes."

"Hello, Johnathan, I used to play soccer when I was in college. You look pretty good out there."

"Thanks, I didn't know they played soccer in college. I thought they only did football and basketball."

Clair smiled at him. "I was telling your dad that a lot of good colleges have soccer teams and are looking for good players and even give scholarships. I can give your dad a list of colleges if you'd like."

"I'm only in middle school. I've got plenty of time to worry about all that, right?" Johnathan was warming up to the doctor. He liked that she knew about soccer.

Coach Maddox called Johnathan to join the team for the second half of the game. "I gotta go. Bye, Dad," Johnathan hesitated before adding. "Thanks for coming, you too, Dr. Murphy."

The game was a tight one, and Johnathan's team won by one goal.

Helping to fold up their chairs and pack their cooler bag, Murphy said, "Max, that was fun. I haven't been to a kid's game in ages. I'd come again if you'd ask me."

Harlow stopped and looked at the doctor. "I will ask you to come again. I've enjoyed spending time with you, and I think Johnathan liked you too."

Walking back to Harlow's car, they saw his ex-wife coming to pick up Johnathan. "Hello, Carolyn. Jonathan played a great game."

"I'm surprised you found the time," Carolyn said with her hands on her hips. She tilted her head in Murphy's direction.

"Sorry, Carolyn, this is Dr. Clair Murphy, the Sarasota Chief Medical Examiner. We sometimes work cases together. Clair played soccer in college and came with me to see Johnathan play." Why was he defending himself for attending one of his son's games with Dr. Murphy? He tried to hold his temper in check.

"We have to get back," Harlow said, picking up the chairs again.

"It was nice meeting you," Murphy said, trying to be polite.

All she got in return was, "Hmm." Carolyn stomped off to where Johnathan's team was huddled.

"Whoa, that was awkward," Clair said, helping to throw the chairs and the cooler bag in the trunk.

"I'm sorry. Carolyn can be a bit prickly about me spending time with the kids. She's always complaining I don't spend enough with them. I can't seem to get the balance right between being a father and a cop."

They sat in the car with the engine running, waiting for the AC to cool them down.

Clair reached over and took Max's hand. "Divorce is never easy when children are involved."

"You know how it is," replied Max. "When dealing with a case, I can't always drop everything for a game or a school activity. It's not like I have a nine-to-five job." He was getting upset. Furious even that Carolyn couldn't or wouldn't see his side.

He'd been a cop when they met and married. The divorce rate among the police officers was above average because of the hours away from the family. Carolyn said she was prepared to deal with it, but Harlow knew she resented him more and more for being absent while their children were growing up.

"I understand the demands of the job, Max. My husband was a professor at New College. He had his obligations, and I had mine. We worked it out. Not everyone can. He's been gone for several years now, and I still miss the times we talked in the evenings. Rare though they were."

Harlow and Murphy both realized that they were still holding hands.

"How about some lunch?" Max asked, putting the car in reverse. His phone rang as he was backing out. "It's Markowski," he said to Clair. He listened in silence to the call.

"Okay, thanks," Harlow said, hanging up.

"Lenkov called. He wants to meet. I'll have to skip lunch."

They slowly released their hands. "Max, we need to talk about what might be happening here," Clair said, looking Max in the eyes.

Harlow didn't know what was happening, but he liked Murphy. Did he want more?

Chapter Fifty-One

Lenkov was waiting for the detectives in a coffee shop on Second Street in Sarasota. He was nervously stirring his coffee that had long gone cold.

Looking up when Harlow and Markowski entered the shop, Lenkov nodded and waited for them to sit at his table.

"You wanted to see me?" Harlow asked.

"I want to stay alive, and the only way I can do that is to help you put Vassiliev in prison."

"Have you spoken to Vassiliev since you made bail?" Harlow asked.

Markowski went to the counter to order the coffee.

"He welcomed me but was very cold and dismissive. He wasn't happy with me returning. He asked what I had told the police. I told him I didn't say anything about him, but he didn't believe me. Detective Harlow, I'm afraid he'll find a way to assure my silence with regards to his business dealings."

Markowski returned with coffee and two apple pastries. Harlow cocked an eyebrow at his partner.

"Really?"

"I'm hungry," Markowski answered, dumping two sugar packets in his coffee.

"Mr. Lenkov, would you be willing to wear a

wire and get Vassiliev to admit to being a part of this drug operation?" Harlow said.

"I've been thinking of ways to do just that, but I'm afraid he'll discover what's going on. Maybe search me and find the wire. He'll kill me on the spot."

"We'll make sure he doesn't. There will be men posted all around the building. We'll be listening to the whole conversation. If there is any sign of trouble, we'll come in."

Lenkov nodded, "Okay, with Melnikov dead and James Scholfield out of the picture, he'll need to hire a new cook. Maybe I can get him to meet the new one. And, in the process, he will incriminate himself," Lenkov said.

"Mr. Lenkov, we will have to set this up very carefully. You will have to let us know the day, time, and where you plan on meeting Vassiliev. Did you have anyone in mind for your cook?"

"Not yet. I don't know anyone with the skills to convince Vassiliev. The person would have to know how to cook meth and the precautions to take. It can't be just any addict of the street. Vassiliev would know it was a setup."

"Right," Harlow said. His sharp mind was already thinking of someone who knew chemicals and the dangers of cooking meth, but would she do it? Could he put her at risk like that?

Markowski took their empty plates and cups to the counter, ordering half a dozen pastries to take back to the office. He was thin as a rail and could afford to eat the sugary sweets.

Harlow was pre-diabetic, and try as he might, he couldn't resist the occasional sweet treat. Markowski would get an earful for buying them.

Returning to the table, Markowski said. "Max, are you thinking what I'm thinking?"

"Yep," Harlow said. They had some planning to do to pull off arresting Vassiliev. He was slippery. Was he connected to bigger fish in Russia? Did he have diplomatic connections? They'd have to map this carefully. He was oily and could slip away any day or night.

"Don't do anything stupid and be careful around Vassiliev. We'll call you when we have a plan in place." Harlow stood to leave.

Lenkov nodded, taking a deep breath. "My life is in your hands if I help you."

"I remember," Harlow said as they left Lenkov.

Chapter Fifty-Two

Harlow was at the shooting range, getting in some well-needed practice. His targets showed he needed it. He was thinking about what he was about to ask Murphy to do. He didn't know of anyone else who could pull it off. She could say no. She should say no. It was dangerous He didn't think she would. Did they want to risk her life? Did he have a choice? He told himself to let Clair make the decision. He punched in her number.

"Hey, Murph. Can you meet me for lunch? I have an idea I'd like to run by you." Harlow tried to sound casual.

"Okay, meet me in half an hour at Duval's. You're paying." Clair hung up, chuckling to herself. She could have opted for the station café again, but she wanted Max out of his comfort zone. Besides, she had skipped breakfast and was starving, and cafeteria food would not cut it. She would have to leave now and hope for a parking space.

Harlow had to hunt for a spot and arrived fifteen minutes late. Murphy was already sitting at a table with an iced tea in hand.

The server came over to take their order. Murphy ordered a small fish and chips. After the pastry with Lenkov at the coffee shop and another at his desk, Harlow played it safe. He ordered a salad.

"Okay, what are you up to? You wanted to talk about an idea you had. I have a feeling I'm not going to like it," Clair said.

Max cleared his throat. "You know that Lenkov murdered Melnikov. He's agreed to help up bring down Vassiliev and his drug operation. In exchange, the commander and I have talked with the DA about a plea deal. There is no doubt that he will be convicted of the murder. Lenkov will get life instead of the chair."

"So, what's your idea?"

"Vassiliev needs a new meth cook. It came to me that you could apply for the job."

Her voice dropped open. "Are you out of your tiny little mind?" Murphy sputtered, choking on her tea.

The server put their dishes in front of them. "You okay, ma'am?"

"Yes, I'm fine, thanks. The tea went down the wrong way."

When she left, Max continued. "Lenkov has agreed to wear a wire. We get Vassiliev to the cook house with you and Lenkov. Several leading questions from you and Lenkov could make Vassiliev trap himself."

"What protection do I have if this idea of yours goes sideways? I'm not ready to die so that you can arrest some villain."

"We'll have a team close by, listening. As soon as Vassiliev says enough to bring to the DA for prosecution, we'll charge in and arrest him."

"Shit, Harlow," she said, reverting back to his last name. "You do know how to treat a girl. I had a wild thought that you were going to ask me to go away for a weekend or at least on a proper date. Instead, you want me to pretend to be a meth cook and maybe get killed." Murphy stopped eating and played with her food, smashing her French fries into mashed potatoes.

"The SWAT team will be right there. The danger is minimum."

"Who are you trying to convince? Me or yourself?"

"Both, I think." Harlow reached across to take her hand. "I'm not asking this lightly. I need someone who can convince Vassiliev. Someone who knows drugs. The street talk. It has to happen quickly before any more people die from this damn drug."

Clair didn't answer right away. Was she out of her mind? "Okay, I'll do it. But if I get killed, I'll never speak to you again. You have to let me on every little detail." She pushed her half-eaten meal away.

"Clair, did you mean it when you said you thought I was going to ask you to go away for the weekend? Or on a real date?"

Murphy tilted her head and bit her lower lip before she answered. "Yes, I was rather hoping you might. If you did ask me to go away with you or on a date, I might even say yes to either proposal. I'm too old to beat around the bush, Max. I like you."

"I like you too, Clair," Harlow said, pushing his plate away.

"Shut up and listen, Max, while I still have the courage." Murphy said, rolling her napkin in her hands.

"I'm very happy when we're together, and it's been a long time since I felt comfortable being with someone enough to contemplate dating again, not to mention spending a weekend away with them."

Harlow's heart was beating so hard he could hear it. Murphy was blushing after such a bold statement. They both felt like teenagers navigating those first few awkward encounters of dating angst.

Their meals finished; Harlow paid the bill. "I'd

like to take you out on a proper date, Clair. I've been afraid you might say no, and I'd feel like an idiot."

"Max, you are a sweet and kind man. After this is all over, let's plan on something to celebrate. That is if I'm still alive," Murphy said, trying to lighten the mood but not quite making it.

"I like that. Let's get back and end this."

Chapter Fifty-Three

Markowski watched Harlow walk into the squad room. "Did you ask Murphy to help with Vassiliev?"

"Yeah, I did," Harlow said, throwing his hat on his littered desk.

"Well, what did she say? Is she going to do it?"

"She said she would do it. I've got to tell you I'm not happy about using Dr. Murphy, but we don't have time to find anyone else who can do it. There are a lot of moving pieces to this operation. I have to talk to Commander Robinson to get the go-ahead. The SWAT guys will need to be on board. I should call the sheriff's department for some backup as well."

Harlow shuffled over to the small coffee area in the squad room and made himself a cup of stale coffee. He had trouble ignoring the box of donuts someone had brought in.

Taking his cup back to his desk, he sat across from Markowski. "We need to get with Lenkov again and find out if and where they have set up the new cook house. This operation rests on how convincing Lenkov can be. And if he can get Vassiliev to the cook house. If this goes south, Lenkov and Murphy could both get killed."

"Max, there will be plenty of our officers around close by. We'll be able to hear every word they say. If there is the least thing that sounds like Lenkov or Murphy is in trouble, we'll be there," Markowski said, trying to convince Harlow and himself that things would work out.

Harlow and Markowski spent the next few hours making phone calls and putting their plan together. The sooner they had the location of the cook house, the better.

It was just after five o'clock when Harlow's phone rang.

He put it on speaker so Markowski could hear. It was Lenkov.

"Vassiliev has arranged for the cook house to be in an old, abandoned house off Osprey Lane in south Sarasota near the hospital. He had some goons chase off some squatters living there and moved in a bunch of equipment.

"I told him I found a new cook, and he wants to set up a meet. He asked a lot of questions, like how I found the cook and did he know what he was doing. I can tell you he's not happy. Vassiliev's paranoia is running overtime. I hope whoever you have doing this knows what they are getting themselves in for."

Harlow wondered the same thing. He was risking Murphy's life.

Chapter Fifty-Four

Murphy met Lenkov at the small shopping mall across from the Sarasota Memorial Hospital. Harlow and Markowski sat in their car watching from a distance sipping Starbucks coffee.

"Hello, Mr. Lenkov, I'm Clair Murphy," Murphy said, slipping into the passenger seat of his BMW. "Nice ride you have here."

"I was paid well for my services," Lenkov replied. "I didn't expect a woman. I also expected a younger person. Aren't you a little old to be doing something like this?"

"With age comes wisdom and knowledge." Murphy was quaking inside but refused to let Lenkov see her fear at what she was about to do. She had dressed the part of someone from the streets: worn jeans, a soiled button-down shirt in a tropical design, an old canvas hat, dirty sneakers.

"Let's get this over with," Murphy urged. "Where are we going?"

"It's not far," Lenkov said, starting the engine. He turned onto Tamiami Trail and up Hillview Avenue to the McClellan Park area. He parked in front of a small wooden house with boarded-up windows and a tattered sign that read, *Keep Out No Trespassing*.

Murphy thought a good gust of wind would blow the place down, never mind a hurricane. The house had probably been abandoned for years, and no one in their right mind would buy it.

"Come on," Lenkov said, opening his door and stepping out. He didn't wait for Murphy and walked quickly up the side of the house to the back door.

Murphy caught up to him as he opened the back door. The stench of the chemicals inside mixed with the dank, musty smell of the old house. She imagined the black mold creeping up the walls in the Florida humidity. Murphy slipped a mask out of her purse. She knew the dangers of black mold, never mind the chemicals in the house.

Murphy followed Lenkov to what might have been the dining room. Spread out on folding tables were bags of ephedrine, hotplates, large pots, all the ingredients for cooking meth. Spread on another table: sealable sandwich bags, plastic wraps, gallon bottles, trash bags, rolls and rolls of tape, and more for distribution of the product. In front of Murphy were all the items necessary for making the meth that would be mixed with the heroin to make bath salts — a lethal drug cocktail.

Lenkov checked his watch as they heard a car stop and doors slam.

Murphy tried her calm herself. Her heart was racing. *God, what have I gotten myself into this time? Please just let me live through it.*

Footsteps echoed as someone approached. Murphy had a realization. She had heard two car doors slam and now two sets of footsteps.

Vassiliev entered the room, smartly dressed and sophisticated. A woman was with him. She dangled on Vassiliev's arm, looking like she popped off the pages of SRQ Magazine

The woman had a familiar face. Where had Murphy seen her before? Courthouse? Soccer fields? Grocery store?

If she recognized Murphy as the Sarasota coroner, it could be fatal. Murphy tried to think if the woman had met her before. If she was recognized, she was dead.

Chapter Fifty-Five

Harlow had seen Vassiliev, and Anya Melnikov enter the house. "What the hell is she doing here? Melnikov's wife said she didn't know anything. Swore she wasn't involved in what her husband was up to."

"Well, apparently, she lied. And we believed her," Markowski said. "We have to wait this out and see how it plays."

Harlow looked in his rear mirror and saw the police van parked down the block with its receiving equipment. Murphy was wearing the wire instead of Lenkov. It was a small transmitter that looked like a button on her shirt.

Harlow and Markowski quietly left their car and joined the team in the van. Looking around the area, Harlow could see plainclothes officers strategically placed. A crew was patching a sewer line. Two younger officers were riding skateboards, and a jogger sprinted along the palm-shaded street. A helicopter circled overhead, and SWAT members were poised. All the team members were in place.

The receiver crackled. Someone was talking.

"What is she doing here?" Lenkov shouted, directing his anger at Vassiliev and Anya.

"Did you really think I was letting you run this

operation all by yourself? Anya has been filling me in on things this whole time."

Anya chuckled, "All those times in bed when you told me how you would like to be the head of the operation, I had to keep from laughing. You don't have the balls," she sneered.

Lenkov lunged at Anya. He wanted to rip her lying throat out. Vassiliev pulled out a SIG-Sauer 9 mm semiautomatic pistol tucked in his waistband. He aimed at Lenkov. From five feet, he couldn't miss.

"Now, now none of that. We have a job to do. Introduce me to your guest."

Murphy was wide-eyed. She swallowed and took a breath, not realizing she had been holding it.

"This is the new cook," Lenkov said.

"You have got to be kidding me. This old woman can't possibly know how to cook meth," Vassiliev said. He looked Murphy over.

Bristling, Murphy had to save the operation. "Watch who you're calling *old*. I can cook!"

"What makes you think you're able to cook meth?" Vassiliev challenged.

"I was a pharmacist in the Navy and know chemicals and how to mix them. Young folks don't know everything. I'm careful and make a good product. I got tired of the cold weather up north and hitched down here. Homeless and on the move in Sarasota."

"I want you to cook some meth for me. Make the bath salts, and then we will see if I will employ you."

She stepped forward, hands in pockets so their shaking would not betray her.

"The crap that another idiot was making was not good for business. So, I had Lenkov dispose of him. If someone dies from the bath salts, he cannot buy again. I want repeat business."

They had Vassiliev. The whole operation was

recorded. Yanking off his headphones, Harlow signaled to the officers: move in.

Chapter Fifty-Six

The SWAT team quickly surrounded the crack house. Harlow and Markowski paused for them to breach the back door. He cautiously approached with Markowski, guns drawn, listening for sounds inside.

Following the SWAT team, Harlow entered the room where Vassiliev, Anya Melnikov , Lenkov, and Murphy stood.

It was a stalemate. Guns were drawn and pointed everywhere. "Bastard," Vassiliev shouted. He shot Lenkov, hitting him in the chest. Lenkov went down, groaning at Murphy's feet.

The bullet had punctured a major artery, and he was losing blood rapidly. Murphy tried to stanch the flow of blood. She could tell Lenkov was not likely to make it.

Vassiliev grabbed Anya as a shield, "Move out of my way, or I'll kill her."

"Now, why would you want to do that? The house is surrounded, and there is no way out. Even if you kill her, there is no way out," said Harlow. "Save yourself and give up before anyone else gets hurt. You can't win this one, Vassiliev. We have you on tape."

"Lenkov betrayed me."

Anya Melnikov was struggling to free herself

from Vassiliev's grip. "Let me go, Alexie. I had nothing to do with this. It was Lenkov. He wanted to take over the business and run the operation. Please, Alexie."

"You lying little bitch," Vassiliev sneered. "You played both of us." Vassiliev pushed her away. He shot her between the eyes, then held up his hands, tossing the gun away, smiling, "No one betrays me and gets away with it."

Markowski rushed in to grab and subdue Vassiliev.

"Well, what do we have here?" Markowski said, pulling a small Smith and Weston pistol from his right ankle. He handed him over to officers who would bring him to the station.

Harlow kneeled beside Murphy, who was on the floor beside Lenkov. Her bloody hands were pressing on Lenkov's chest, trying to stem the blood flow. Lenkov's head suddenly dropped to the side as he died.

Murphy looked up into the eyes of the officers jammed into the room. Hazmat was standing by to secure the drug lab.

"You okay? Come on, Clair, he's gone." Harlow helped Murphy to stand. She leaned on him for support, shocked and crying silently. Two bodies lay on the floor.

"I will be okay."

Paramedics took Murphy and sat her down, checking her vitals, giving her some water. They cleaned up her hands.

Murphy saw that Lenkov's blood was still under her nails and embedded in the creases of her shaking hands.

Shaking off the paramedics, Murphy turned to Harlow. "Take me home, Max."

Chapter Fifty-Seven

Harlow left Markowski in charge of winding up the operation and securing the scene.

Commander Robinson strolled over. "Well done, Max. You and the team did a good job here today."

"Thank you, sir," a weary Harlow answered.

Harlow drove Murphy back to his house. She needed to shower and change her blood-stained clothes. Harlow handed her a sweatshirt and jogging pants.

He poured them both a large tumbler of whiskey.

Clair entered the room, rubbing a towel over her dripping hair. "I didn't find a hairdryer."

Harlow smiled and ran his hand over his short gray hair, "I don't need one," he said, handing her the whiskey.

"Thanks. I earned it." Murphy collapsed on the worn sofa. "I never saw someone die like that. Anya Melnikov too. I'm happy to work with them when they are already dead."

Clair let a tear escape as Max sat beside her and put his arm around her shoulder, pulling her close.

"What you did today will save a lot of lives. Vassiliev will go to prison for his crimes, and some lethal drugs are out of our neighborhoods."

"Lenkov also tried to do the right thing at the

end and lost his life for it."

"Yes, he did in the end, but remember he pushed drugs and murdered Melnikov. He was on a very destructive path."

"Listen, why don't you call in one of your assistants to do the autopsies on Lenkov and Melnikov? Take a few days off, if your boss will let you."

"Hey, I'm the chief medical examiner. I'll decide if I take time off or not."

"I'm just saying you have been through a lot."

"I'm fine, Max," she said. Clair paused to catch her breath and decide what she wanted to say. She turned to look at Max. "Remember, you said something about going away for a weekend sometime?"

"Yeah, I remember something about that."

"I want to go now. Right away." She reached up to caress his rough face.

"St. Augustine? Or the Keys?"

"Perfect, you pick. But, in the morning," Clair took Max's hand and drew him to her. He kissed her gently and guided her down the hall to his room, still holding her hand.

Acknowledgement

I wish to thank my content editor, Mark Mathes,
for his help with police procedures and keeping me
on the right track. I also want to thank my copy editor,
Joanne Tailele, for spotting all the things I missed.
A very special thank you goes to fellow author,
mentor and friend, DL Havlin,
for all his advise and encouragement.

About the Author

Brenda M. Spalding is a prolific, award-winning author and is often called upon to speak at book clubs, conferences, and writers' groups. Originally from Massachusetts, she now live in Bradenton, Florida. She is the past president of the National League of American Pen Women- Sarasota Branch, a member of the Sarasota Authors Connection, Sarasota Fiction Writers, Florida Authors and Publishers, and a co-founding member and current president of ABC Books Inc.

www.bradenriverconsulting.com
bradenriverconsulting@gmail.com
www.Heritagepublishingus.com
spaldingauthor@gmail.com

Made in the USA
Columbia, SC
16 October 2022

69508958R00089